John Hill

Treason-felony

Vol. I

John Hill

Treason-felony
Vol. I

ISBN/EAN: 9783337052973

Printed in Europe, USA, Canada, Australia, Japan

Cover: Foto ©Andreas Hilbeck / pixelio.de

More available books at **www.hansebooks.com**

A Novel

BY

JOHN HILL

AUTHOR OF

'SALLY,' 'THE CORSARS,' 'AN UNFORTUNATE ARRANGEMENT,' ETC.

IN TWO VOLUMES

VOL. I.

London

CHATTO & WINDUS, PICCADILLY

1892

CONTENTS OF VOL. I.

TREASON-FELONY

CHAPTER I.

THREE GENTLEMEN ADVENTURERS.

THE Republic known as the Estados Unidos d'Eldorado has for its immediate neighbour the Republic known as the Confederated Guano Free States. The two countries have a continuous sea-board on the ocean, which may be called the Atlific or Pacantic, Eldorado being north of Guano on the South American coast, and their neighbouring and surrounding States on the landward side are Porquezuela, Piguador, Papagay, the Coprolite

Republic, and Balliragua. Having for some time past obtained loans from confiding European investors, on the strength of beautifully-fashioned, persuasive statistics, in which their inexhaustible natural wealth in wool, hides, meat, bones, maize, horses, copperas, manure, linseed-oil, silver, and other sundry matters, was set glowingly forth, as well as the immense future possibility of fertile tracts of great extent, which as yet lay inviting the emigrant to cultivate them, which would grow everything in the world by being merely looked at, both countries expended the money obtained in useful and productive public works, as they had undertaken to do, viz., on the latest things in the cruiser and gunboat line, on ammunition, uniforms, and Winchester repeaters. A further sum was usefully employed in building *quintas* for local contractors, and enlarging the salaries of all the

Government officials from the respective Presidents, General Nitre and Dr. Solomon Ladron, down-wards and laterally. If anything was left after that, it was used, as long as it lasted, for paying the interest on the debt.

Having got all these things, the next obvious thing to do was to go to war, if only from a child-like desire to let off their new guns; and to war they went, something near ten years ago.

The world at large was not deeply interested in this fell collision, nor was the course of history expected to be gravely altered by it; but at the same time there was some very pretty fighting occasionally, and a good deal of miscellaneous plunder picked up by bold and ingenious persons belonging to the not yet wholly extinct order of soldiers of fortune.

We are to give our more immediate attention,

for a little while, to the cruiser *Infierno y Tomasito,* of the Eldorado navy, which was pursuing its way southward one fine morning, just within sight of the coast, on the look-out, primarily, for the *Almirante McCarthy,* of the hostile navy, and, secondarily, for any mischief which might turn up.

The weather was warm, the sea calm, and the air clear, so that the remote outlines of rising ground behind the shore-line were more distinctly visible than they would have been at that distance in the hazier atmosphere of an English summer morning.

On the bridge stood three officers—two in naval, and the third in a military uniform; the uniform, in fact, of a colonel of the Estada Mayor of Eldorado.. The taller and older of the two naval officers was scanning the horizon with a telescope, being no less a man than the Señor Capitan Don Miguel

Doherty, whose rich Castilian accents might have been heard to say:

'Now, where in the wide sea is that old hooker trying to Kinsale herself?'

'She's generally handy when there's a row to be had for the asking, too,' replied the Señor 'Teniente Patrick Vane.

'Why are we not taking advantage of her absence,' inquired the Señor Coronel Comandante Ronald Macgregor, 'to take San José?'

San José del Estercolero was the first town on the Guano coast which would be passed by anyone going from the north southwards.

'That's what I'm asking myself,' replied Captain Doherty; 'and if we get so far without interruption, we'll have a look at the place. I think we ought to get a pretty steep ransom out of them by merely showing ourselves, but if not, we'll land

and take it. And that'll be a job for your boys,
Macgregor.'

'My boys are just the choicest collection of
picturesque picaroons and marauding murderers,
I ever had the honour of commanding, which is
no small thing for me to say. But I've an idea.
that they'll fight. I've drilled them, in close and
extended order, till they're fit to parade before
Moltke, and I've told them that I will shoot then
and there any man who skulks in the attack, so
that it will be mohr creditable to let the enemy do
it if they're to be shot at all. I found that pay
with the Serbs.'

'Well, I guess we'll go below and have breakfast,' said Captain Doherty. 'It's 'Teniente
Enrique Santos' turn to navigate and keep a look
out, and it'll be some time before we see San
José.'

And they went down to a very comfortably-appointed cabin, which was all paid for, down to the varnished maple panelling and gilding and white paint, by European investors, now daily engaged in anxious study of the sinking quotations of the Eldorado Unified Eight per Cent. External Loan. During the meal, it may be well to give a general impression of the aspect of the three, as there was no conversation to report till the eating and drinking was over—the eating, at any rate.

Doherty was about forty, looking as strong, tall, hard, and bright as a lighthouse, as Vane said. He had a round, closely-cropped head, strong square jaws, a prominent chin, a thick, close brown moustache, a rather snub nose, small keen blue eyes, and a sun-and-wind-tanned skin. When he was not eating or drinking, he was always screwing half a cigar about in the corner of his mouth, and you would have taken him immediately for an American, if you had chanced to meet him anywhere, until he opened his mouth and spoke. Even then he would occasionally use an American form of words or simile, though in the imperishable accent of the land he was born in.

Vane was about the same age, or, maybe, a year or two younger, was rather below the middle height, had a handsome aquiline face, big well-set blue eyes, with a laugh in them, reddish-brown hair, and a long red sweeping moustache. His skin was burnt a bricky red, as is usual in fair men exposed to sun and wind.

Macgregor was taller than Vane, and less heavily built than Doherty. Of the three Celtic gentlemen, he was of the darkest type. He had a lean frame and a sombre face, with somewhat bony features, including a high thin nose, long jaw, high cheekbones, and gray eyes, set in deep orbits, under arched black brows. He had black hair, a slender black wisp of moustache, all length and no thickness, and a tawny brown skin, which had been sallow before the sun gilded it and exposure darkened it. His age was about thirty-five.

After breakfast had been eaten, each poured himself out a glass of *aguardiente*, the substitute for whisky in that part of the world, and lit his pipe, cigar, or cigarette. Doherty smoked a cigar, Macgregor a blackened wooden pipe, and Vane, who was dandified and fond of the society of ladies, a cigarette.

'Here is fortune to us all, gentlemen,' said Captain Doherty, lifting his glass. 'Pat, can't you give us a bit of a song?'

'Later on. I want to get into the right frame of

mind first. Queer thing, isn't it, us three finding ourselves together again in a concern of this kind?'

'We've been in some steep places together before now, any way,' replied Doherty, ' haven't we, Mac?'

'Ay; together—and separately.'

'Mike, have you told Mac what we're going to do if we get well out of this?'

'I have not.'

'Then, why are you not doing it now? Sure we know him.'

'Some insane treason, I suppose,' observed Macgregor calmly; ' seize the ship, and run away with her, bombard London, or do something equally practical with the harp without the crown, and the wolf-dog lying down in it somewhere.'

Macgregor had a cool, deliberate manner, and something of a Western Scotch accent, which gave character and emphasis to his irony.

' Some insane treason, you may take your oath,'
said Vane, ' though not quite such a fool's trick as
you're after describing. My boy, we'll have
Ireland in a blaze one of these fine days! There,
it's making me drop into powutry. Will I tell
him, Mike?'

' You're after telling so much already that you'd
better make it complete. Of course, Mac's all
right, but he'll only think us a couple of fools old
enough to know better.'

' Listen now, Mac, while I tell you. You know
Mike's been home?'

' I did not know it; but it's like his infernal
cheek.'

' Isn't it? when there's an unpaid debt to the
British Empire of twenty years' penal servitude
still owing from him!'

' Pat, it takes more intellect than I possess to

grasp how a person can owe a debt that is otherwise than unpaid,' observed Macgregor dryly and deliberately.

Doherty chuckled grimly and chewed his cigar.

'Ah now, don't trifle with me, you great long Scotch skeleton at a banquet! If it comes to a contest of wits, I can give you away any day. You're only pedantic. Well, as I was saying, Mike's been back to old Ireland, God save her! and organizing and arranging for correspondence, and the like of that, and devil a peeler knew him, and no wonder! He hasn't been there since '66, or thereabouts, and a new generation of peelers has risen since then. Of course, the boys are all drilling in the glens of a summer night as usual, and there's all the usual conspiracies, with passwords and signs and informers, and single-barrelled slug-slingers, and the rest of it; and what Mike has had to do to begin with, is to devise some game that will not have the weak points about it which spoilt things in the old days. Now, what were those weak points?'

Pat Vane had only paused oratorically, and intended to reply to his own question, but Macgregor answered without hesitation :

' Hopeless incapacity on the part of your leaders, as a rule !'

' Now, I traverse that. The world has not made better leaders of men than some who came from Ireland, or better followers of leaders, either. Look at the English army. Mostly Irish—God forgive them all! Look at Uncle Sam's army. Irish, when not German or nigger. Your money-making, selfish, prosaic, common-sense, constitutional, unemotional prig of a Sassenach has a wonderful talent for getting the Celts to do all the fighting for him, and then growling over the expense. All that good material and energy wasted on England and America! My boy, if it was properly applied and directed, Ireland would not only be free and independent, but would be a first-class European Power, which Continental nations would respect and appreciate, instead of hating and ridiculing, as they do old Pounds and Pence and Piety, which would then assume its proper and suitable position, which is about that of Holland.'

'This is very entertaining, Pat, but a bit parenthetic. If there is a point whatever, wouldn't it be well to come to it?'

'Dry up, Pat,' said Captain Doherty, removing his cigar and spitting cleverly into the brass cuspidor. 'Mac doesn't want to hear you rave about Ireland's potential splendour, but how we're to start getting

instalments of it. It is the fact that I've been to
Ireland certainly, and got away again without any
particular trouble. As Pat Vane says, the usual
things were going on, and likely to lead to the
usual arrests, trials, jury-packings, Coercion Acts,
and rewards for peelers, spies and informers, payable in the form of rates and taxes by the popula-
tion, or the de-population. What I want to get
up is something that won't end in a fizzle. You
know me, Mac : when we first met among Garibaldi's
red shirts, I was just on the skip from my first
go-in at the British Empire, and had acquired
some elementary ideas of military matters on the
Potomac, and in the neighbourhood of Richmond.
But I've learned a lot since then. I've seen modern
European tactics, with long-range weapons around
Orleans, under Aurelle de Paladine, and, later, with
the Carlistas, as well as over here, as you know,

and I'm not likely to believe in casual " risings " of
dunderheaded mobs.   You will allow that I know
what I'm talking about.   And I don't undervalue
English troops.   I saw too much of them ·not so
long ago, on the trail for Candahar, to do that.
Though, to be sure, their leader was Irish, and
the best of the troops Scotch and Irish, in that
particular crowd.'

' Were you there, too, ye daft old ruffian ?'

' Only came from there a few months ago.   I
was corresponding for the *Chicago Sunburst*, if anybody happened to spot me, and had credentials to
that effect on my person.'

' You've the cheek of Niel O'Hea,' observed
Vane.

' What did he do, Pat ?' asked Macgregor.

' When they let him out, after he'd done his time
for T. F., he offered to bet the governor that hell

was pleasanter than Portland, and proposed to toss up which should go and see.'

' Well, Doherty, man, proceed with your plan.'

' To begin with, Ireland's the wrong place to work in. Too many peelers and uniforms about, making a living out of second-hand two-cent plots, and explosions in drainpipes and canned-meat tins. I want a headquarters in a quiet place which will be quite free from suspicion, and, at the same time, within easy reach of Ireland. I want a lonely country house, standing in its own grounds, haunted for choice, with access to the sea, and some miles from a railway-station. I rather calculate a yacht would come in handy, too. Somewhere in the South-west of England, where no one but tourists, invalids, and artists would want to come, either in the Bristol Channel or the other. Vane's got the place in his eye. I know little or

nothing personally about England as a place
to live in, having never lived there. Now, the
strategical advantages of this are, privacy; access-
ibility in one way, viz., by water; inaccessibility
by rail—I mean that there would be plenty of time
to dig out if necessary, in case of alarm—and
above all, absence of suspicion. Then we would
have over small batches of suitable and proper
young men, each to spend a certain time in being
taught his duties properly—for instance, we could
do skeleton drill, extended order, and attack forma-
tion in the grounds—and when they were done
with, we'd send 'em home, and get over another
lot. They should have lectures on tactics, with
illustrations from the lecturer's experiences, from
recent history, and from a *Krieg-spiel* we'd get
up with a sand-relief map. You can vary the
country as much as you like with a sand model,

and a drop or two of water to bind it. Then we'd
hold examinations, and qualify them accordingly,
as non-commissioned officers or as company
officers, as the case might be. It would be a
regular Staff College. Might even let the neighbours know we took pupils, but perhaps better
not. We'd have departments—one to be com-
mandant, one to take field and permanent works,
one tactics, another drill and manœuvre, and
so on.'

' This will cost many shekels, my friend.'

' There's lots of funds collecting in the United
States which are being forwarded to Heffernan in
Paris. If he finds Paris too full of wasps to hold
him, he'll go to Amsterdam. And I've placed the
right men in different parts of Ireland to select the
boys, and send them over to the Staff College to be
ground into something more useful than faction-

leaders and football-players. Besides, Vane and I stand to win a fair lot of loot in this business we're in now, and we'll devote that to it, of course.'

'Oh, it's great! Mac, you ought to be in it, for the sake of old times. Besides, we'll make you a General of Division when the great sunburst comes.'

'Easy now. Mac is no Englishman or informer, but, at the same time, we have no right to ask him to put his head in the lion's mouth, for that's what it comes to (referring, of course, to the lion usually found in association with a unicorn). Still, he knows how welcome he would be if he saw his way to give his services to Ireland.'

Macgregor replied:

'I'm in the habit of selling my sword to anyone with whom I can honourably sympathize, provided I am properly paid for it. Being by family and

by conviction of Legitimist views, I fought for Don
Carlos at a reduction, and hold from his Majesty,
the lawful King of France and Spain, the rank of
Captain-General in consequence. Being descended
from outlawed, murdered, and persecuted Jacobite
ancestors, I have no special prejudice in favour of
the Hanoverian monarchy. Moreover, I am suffi-
ciently acquainted with the history of the relations
between England and Ireland to have no con-
scientious objection to the latter levying war on
the former, though I may perceive practical difficulties in the way of bringing such war to a
successful issue. Finally, and very briefly, as the
Presbyterian ministers say, is a salary attached
to your Staff College? And, in conclusion, what
might it be expected to amount to in lawful
currency?'

Doherty rose silently, and held out his hand to

Macgregor, and shook it with the hearty and solemn wrench of an American deputation.

Then Vane said :

'You're a long-winded old fraud, Mac, with a bonnet full of bees and a head full of maggots, but you've got the sand. I knew you wouldn't leave us two to do any fun alone by ourselves. Us three against creation.'

And Vane drained his glass.

'Any way,' said Doherty, 'it's us three against the British Empire, and that's something to work our teeth on. We can give our attention to correcting the flaws of creation afterwards, if we have sufficient leisure.'

'Now I'll give you a song,' said Vane.

I.

'"There is a land across the sea
That dreams of days when it was free,

Where mighty heroes were of old,
And minstrels sang to harps of gold ;
Where maidens grew, all pure and fair—
One day we'll raise a kingdom there."

Chorus, boys :

' " Then think again of Ireland,
    And drink again to Ireland ;
One day we'll stand, with sword in hand,
    To die for dear old Ireland !

II.

' " An end will come of our long night,
    The dark will make our dawn more bright,
    And we will gather back the best
    Of our sons scattered through the West ;
    In our fair island in the sea
    A Nation shall the nations see.

' " Then think again of Ireland,
    And drink again to Ireland,
Until the Green again is seen
    Above the Red in Ireland." '

'Bully for you, Vane,' said Doherty. 'Have you anything to say, Mac, by way of criticism on my Staff College? Your opinion is invited.'

Macgregor drew close to the table, and put his elbows on it, and leaned forwards towards the two, who also approached their faces with serious attention, for they knew that Macgregor, though given to pedantic sarcasm, was a soldier whose experience was great, and valour and skill undoubted. While he is delivering his views, which are perhaps a little too lengthy and too technical to entertain the reader, it may be desirable to give a brief outline of the career of Ronald Macgregor, at present colonel on the Eldorado Staff, and commanding the military force of that State despatched on board the *Infierno y Tomasito.*

He was born in Scotland in 1845 of a family of small means and long pedigree, several members of which had suffered about a century before at Hairibee, while others, at the same time, had lost their estates, and gone into exile and foreign service. In 1864, while a student at Glasgow, he got into trouble with the law, and had to fly the country. The nature of the trouble was more discreditable to his temper and respect for the Queen's peace than to his honour, for it involved homicide, committed on a man who had insulted a girl to whom Macgregor was at the time attached. So he took refuge with members of his family, settled for a generation or two past in Austria, and obtained a commission as second-lieutenant in a regiment of foot, in which capacity he was honourably defeated with Benedek in 1866. After that he went to Italy, and joined Garibaldi, where he met Captain Mike Doherty, who not only had the recent laurels of the 51st Massachusetts clinging to his brow, but had just been trying to organize a 'good healthy rising' in Ireland, of which the issue was a skirmish or two with police and dragoons, a few trials and sentences and hangings, and the flight over sea of Captain Doherty, after hiding in the hills for a week. Vane came with Doherty, but got into difficulties with his conscience, as it occurred to him that he would be fighting to all intents and purposes against the Holy Father, so he went away and offered his sword to the Pontifical Zouaves, or some such body, and was not seen again by the other two till they all met again (happily on the same side), a few years later, fighting in white *berets* for Don Carlos. In that war Macgregor was wounded for the first time, at Cartagena. Afterwards he went on the staff of General Tchernayeff in the Servian War, while Doherty and Vane were engaged in

different South American 'shindies,' where they
picked up some nautical experience, both having
been at all times fairly at home on the sea, and
made themselves useful sometimes on land and
sometimes on water.

This brings us down to the time where our story
opens, when the three world-wandering adventurers
found themselves once more together for a common
purpose, and able to talk over old times with
tobacco and grog in the quiet intervals.

Before they had done conferring in the cabin,
information was brought that the town of San
José del Estercolero was in sight, but no ship of
war. Wherefore the three officers ran up on deck,
and orders were given to prepare for action, while
Colonel Macgregor paraded and inspected his
soldiers, saw forty rounds served out to each, and
looked after the water-bottles. The sailors were

in the meantime told off to the two long 4·7-inch quick-firers and the machine-guns. Oh yes! Eldorado liked to have everything modern, scientific, and expensive, you may be sure.

And the ship drew nearer to the shore, and the town of San José lay before them in the clear summer air, white and glittering like a town made of lump sugar, with an ornate tower or two rising here and there above the general level. Behind the town rose sloping hills, on the sides of which white quasi-classical *quintas* began to be visible, scattered among orange and lemon trees, aloes, and prickly pear. On getting near enough, there were distinguishable, not far from the shore, in front of the white, flat-roofed town, with its towers of the cathedral, Bolsa de Comercio, and pillar of La Libertad, and all the rest of it, some low, brown heaped-up lines of extemporized earth-

works, on which was flying the glorious standard
of the Guano Free States, whose device was a
brown triangular mixen *proper*, with a setting
sun behind it, on a field, striped, *vert* and *argent*.
Doherty, looking through his glass, said :

‘ They'll be hurting somebody, if they don't take
care.   They've got some guns mounted there.
They've got a bit of railroad embankment and
erected platforms behind it, I take it.   Luckily it's
easy landing here, and no particular surf to speak
of, I find.   Vane, signal to 'em to haul down that
old rag, or we'll come and do it for them.’

At that moment there came from the brown line
of earthwork on the land a sudden orange flame, a
puff of dense white smoke, a noise like a distant
train snorting in the air, a loud bang, and then
arose a white fountain or two in the water.

‘ Short ! Now half-speed astern a bit, to puzzle

their range-finder. Get La Santissima Madre loaded with a contact-shell and trained on that work.'

The crew had given this name to one of the two guns the ship carried, without any intention of profanity, rather of affection and respect. The battery on shore repeated its performance, resulting in more fountains in the blue waters of the wide Bay of Estercolero.

Then the gun known among the men as the Santissima Madre was let off with a deafening bang, followed by a lesser bang on shore, and a disintegration of the earthwork was visible when the smoke cleared. The crew yelled at this and leaped about. Meanwhile, the *Infierno y Tomasito* went ahead again, approaching the shore more closely, so that the machine-guns could be used with effect, to the great delight of the crowd of

frolicsome desperadoes flattered by the name of
ship's company, who looked on machine-guns as
new and diverting toys, and very soon there was a
continuous 'H—r—r—ong! H—r—r—ong!' from
the Nordenfeldts, and 'Ft! Spat—spat—spat!'
from the Gardners, punctuated at intervals by the
thundering explosion of the Santissima Madre and
her fellow the San Miguel (so called in compliment
to Captain Doherty); in short, as 'Teniente Pat
Vane said, 'There was as noisy an old Donnybrook
as a gentleman could wish for.'

In the meantime, the two field-pieces on shore
had begun to get a little more 'on the target,' and
a shell arrived on board which sent a Nordenfeldt
into smithereens, exploded the hopper, and killed
or wounded half a dozen men.

'Ah now,' said Captain Doherty, 'we'll go and
give 'em hell for that! Give 'em Mary and

Mike till you dismount one of their guns, and then we'll land!'

It was done. Boats approached the shore, covered by the ship's fire, crammed with seamen and soldiers; the former commanded by Vane, the latter by Macgregor. When they landed, the ship had to cease firing, for fear of hitting her own men, as they advanced in extended order across the flat ground between the beach and the ruinous mounds which had been earthworks, and the defenders concentrated the fire of their small arms on the invaders. The latter, in spite of losses, advanced slowly, and fired, certainly not in orderly section volleys, but in a continuous rattling *Schnell-feuer*, which perhaps did not do much execution, but established an encouraging shield of smoke between them and their adversaries. Whenever they lapsed or faltered, the high trumpeting voice of Macgregor was heard by those near him calling in Caledonian Spanish: 'Sobre el enemigo! Volver a la carga!' Then, when they got near enough for the final rush, Macgregor went in front, as calmly as if on a field-day, drew his sword, and commanded:

'Bayonetas encaladas!'

Vane did likewise, but with greater excitement, adding:

'And go in and kill the beggars! God save Ireland (I mean Eldorado)! Hurroo!'

And a wild noise arose, in which the different yells and shouts peculiar to Spaniard, negro, mestizo, Irishman, Italian, and Scotchman combined in one infernal crescendo, as they 'rushed' the position; and after a bayonet engagement of a few minutes, the troops on the other side were bolting for life, while a reserve boat-load of men had doubled up, dragging a Nordenfeldt with them, which they ran round for 'action front,' and pumped frantically at the retreating foe at the rate of 500 rounds a minute, most of which went over the enemy's head and broke windows and knocked spots out of walls.

Vane and Macgregor met on the inside of the captured entrenchment, the former wiping the sweat from his face with his fingers, so as to produce pleasing striations of red and black on his skin, the red being where he smeared off the gunpowder and the black where he left it. Being quite unaware of this, he remarked :

'Well, Mac, you only want a pair of bones to set you up as a nigger.'

''M,' grunted Macgregor, '*you* only want to be in the place you've escaped as yet, to qualify as a first-class copper-sheathed devil. Here's Sergeant

Lee telling me just now that you made him think of Pooro Beng.'

'Oh, get away out of that! Who's got a drink about him?'

'Where's your water-bottle?'

'Here's the bottom of it, hanging upside down to the sling. One of those swine put a bullet through the rest of it.'

'Hurt you?'

'No.'

'Well, here's my bottle.'

Vane came near Macgregor and got into the rather awkward position required for drinking out of another man's slung water-bottle, sucked greedily at it for awhile, choked, spat, and said:

'What pig-wash have you got in it at all?'

'Well, I couldn't get any oatmeal, so I put in some crushed maize and water, with just a handful

of tea-leaves. I don't fight on whisky in a climate
the like of this.'

'And you a Scotchman, too! Ought to be
ashamed of yourself! What's the next move?'

'Seize the telegraph and Banco Nacional. I've
sent on Captain Urquiza to do it, also to get what
vehicles they require, and transport the—er—
ransom and so forth down to the boats.'

'My boys are gone to restore order in the
town.'

'Ay? Just that. To restore order in the town.
Yes; they would do that.'

'Maybe they'll be collecting a few subscriptions
for charitable purposes, and havin' a little rest and
refreshments. They're tired, poor boys! and
they've done very well.'

'And a good many knocked over, too, God rest
their souls! Well, they've done well, as you say.'

'Oh, they're the boys that fear no noise! And they're making it, too,' he added meditatively, as sounds reached them from the town suggesting something between a Cork election and escaped pigs at a fair, interspersed with a shot or two at intervals.

'Come along, Vane!' said Macgregor; 'we must take a walk through the town. They'll be setting something on fire, or getting into some mischief, if we don't look after them. Hullo!'

A gun was fired from the ship, and Captain Doherty signalled:

'Good boys! Make them hurry down with the stuff, and tell them not to get too drunk.'

'Just that,' said Macgregor; 'come away. Sergeant Lee, have you any ammunition?'

'Kekker, Rya.'*

---

* Gipsy = 'No, sir.'

'Then collect thirty rounds or so out of these dead fellows' pouches, and take your rifle and come along with us.'

Sergeant Lee was a tall, wiry, rather handsome man of about forty, an obvious gipsy, though garbed in the uniform of Eldorado, and disguised in gunpowder like the rest.

The two officers walked away, the buttons of their revolver-cases ready undone, in case of need, and Sergeant Lee followed them, with his bayonet fixed and arm sloped. After crossing some dusty waste ground, over which were scattered cut blocks of stone, pieces of decayed boiler sheeting, casks, one or two railway wheels and a pile of sleepers, and the miscellaneous débris usually found in the neighbourhood of wharves, as well as a few corpses, they got into a street which led into a larger street, the Calle 26 Julio; in fact, a boulevard, with wide sidewalks shaded by rows of bitter-orange trees, on which on ordinary occasions the inhabitants used to loiter and *flaner*, and examine the shop-windows under their gaily-coloured awnings. The Calle 26 Julio, like most modern streets in South American towns (and elsewhere), was straight as a lesson in perspective, and its straightness emphasized by a double tram-line along the middle. And here the trams, a few hours before, had jingled merrily up and down, while the butter-carriers and Basque milk-vendors rode about delivering their produce with melodious calls; and the voice was heard of those who hawked white and glittering tinware, also, of course, on horseback, to the time of ' Tach-uèlas !' Everything here is done on horseback: the newspaper is delivered by a man on a horse, the priest goes on a horse to Mass and to take the Viaticum to the dying. Even the dead are sometimes carried on their last journey on a horse.

Later in the day, about sunset, the citizens under ordinary circumstances would bring chairs and sit outside their front doors reading newspapers, smoking *cigarillos*, and discussing excitedly the state of the *bolsa*, the price of gold money, and the war.

But to-day had brought the war itself rather too close to them, with those accompaniments legitimately attached to it, as well as those irregularities and extravagances of conduct and discipline which are occasionally met with in Central and South America, where the peaceful citizen, placed by fortune between the fell incensed points of mighty opposites, is likely to find himself in a singularly disagreeable position. Wherefore the street was empty, save for occasional bands of armed ruffians who called themselves patrols, and were busy breaking open the shops and plundering them of any portable objects of value. As these men (portions of the naval and military forces of Eldorado) never hesitated to put a bayonet into anyone who resisted their 'collecting subscriptions,' the inhabitants shut themselves into their *patios*, or lay on the flat roof out of the way of bullets, consoling themselves with the reflection that they would probably hear of the same thing happening before long in one of the invaders' towns.

Now and then straggling groups of Guano soldiers appeared and fired at the Eldorado forces, who fired back; but as no one took any particular aim, and no one was particularly sober, and the ammunition in the pouches of both parties had been nearly exhausted in the attack on the works, very little harm was done, except to imprudent non-combatants who looked out of windows.

The conduct of the Eldorado forces, both naval and military, was such as would have procured their incontinent suspension to trees under the rules governing war as understood in Europe, at any rate in these days; but as most of the combatants were simply a horde of banditti, containing the picked blackguards and riff-raff of Europe and America, the native liberated criminal, the exotic man who had 'done something' which made his native land uncomfortable for him, and the Indian half-breed and negro, to whom a war unaccompanied by barbarity and plunder was an incomprehensible abstraction, it was out of the question to adopt a system of humane discipline. You might as well try to teach them the logic of Hegel, or the tonic sol-fa system. Fatigue parties occasionally passed bearing their wounded comrades, either on doors they had pulled down or in requisitioned carts.

'They seem to be enjoying themselves fairly well,' observed Colonel Macgregor; 'but there'll just be the devil's own job getting them all on board again.'

'Indeed there will; but Mike Doherty's not the boy to spoil their diversions unless he's obliged. For instance, if the *Almirante McCarthy* turned up on the horizon, there'd be a tidy old scatter down to the boats. But failing any reason for the contrary, he'll let 'em stay ashore for a reasonable time—long enough to sleep themselves sober, any way. There's a pump, glory be to God! Mac, I'll toss you for first.'

And he span a ten-cent nickel of the United States of Eldorado.

'Eagle.'

'Then it's stars.'

And Vane took off his sword and revolver and

his green naval coat with brass buttons, displayed himself in a gray flannel shirt, with a linen collar and front, which he also removed and placed on the pavement beside Sergeant Lee, and proceeded to put his head and neck under the spout of the pump, while Macgregor worked the handle.

'Lord, that's good!' at last he exclaimed, standing up and wringing the water off his arms and head.

'Go on, Mac; it'll dry me to pump on you.'

Macgregor doffed his martial array, and went through a similar performance.

When they were dry and dressed again, they looked quite gentlemanly.

'Now,' said Macgregor, 'let's go and find a *fonda*, or somewhere where we can have about two quarts of wine. Here's a big square—Plaza della Independencia. Of course it would be! There ought to be a good place here, even if Lee has to break open the cellar. We might fish out some-one, and make him show us where the things are.'

'Mac, there's a big church, and the doors are open.'

'Pat, we'll go in. It's a long while since you and I heard Mass last, and drinks will taste better after it.'

'They will. Come along.'

And these two reckless adventurers, who hoped to pocket a large amount of what they euphemisti-cally called the 'ransom' of San José—these two leaders of a band of unscrupulous pirates, in the garb of an 'army' and 'navy,' whose ships, arms, and coals were paid for with stolen money—these two disciplinarians, who calmly strolled, and smoked, and washed while the ruffians under their command were plundering the town and spilling wine in the gutters, walked into the cathedral of San José, bent the knee duly towards the altar, and then knelt, with bent heads, and their caps in their hands, their swords trailing behind them, on the hard, dirty stone floor, among a crowd of rocking, sobbing, terrified women, while the priests and choir went through their office with as much calmness and concentration as if an enemy were not in possession of the town. It is true that the cathedral was a safe refuge. There were but very few of the invaders who would dare commit sacrilege, and if they had wished to do so, their comrades would have restrained them. Inconsistency at times takes curious forms.

The dim light, the scented air, the cool temperature, and the resonant melodious voices, all combined to produce a wonderful contrast to the scenes of heat, noise, violence, dirt, bloodshed, and blazing sunshine they had lately been figuring in; and Macgregor and Vane felt subdued and soothed, and remembered the days when they had studied humane letters, and were almost shaping resolutions to become decent and peaceable members of society, when the service came to an end, and they were allowed to pass out first by the shuddering crowd, who drew back from them as from dangerous animals, and muttered to one another, and pointed at *los enemigos*. They dipped their fingers duly in the holy, but very dirty, water, crossed themselves, and walked again into the sunlit square, where they found Sergeant Lee (who was a heretic) doing sentry outside the porch of the cathedral. The Plaza della Independencia is a large square, with an elaborate marble fountain in the middle, three tiers high, marble benches at intervals under the trees, large stately houses with ornate balustrades round their flat roofs, and an air of some prosperity and taste, though, of course, the real wealth or beauty of such dwellings could only be judged by a visit to the inside. These houses are usually plain flat blocks outside, but when you have penetrated to the *patio* un-expected visions of comfort, elegance, even opulence, often meet your eye. In this square some of the richest inhabitants of San José have dwellings (though the country *quinta* on the hillside beyond the town is preferred by most), and in this square was an institution known as the English Club, where a few unmistakable Britons were grouped in basket-chairs under an awning, taking brandy-and-soda with their usual indifference to the climate or habits of a foreign land, and, it may be added, their usual indifference to whether the country was at war or not, or, if so, with whom. If their houses or property were molested, they intimated that an application to the British Consul would ensue, resulting in gunboats and unpleasantness. They had nothing to do with Guano politics; all they wanted was to make money, wear flannel trousers, drink brandy-and-soda, and go to the Anglican service at eleven on Sundays, and the affairs of the natives (who were, after all, in their own country, where they must be conceded a right to exist) were wholly irrelevant.

Some of the English omitted to make the money, and some omitted to frequent the Anglican service, but they were unanimous about the brandy-and-soda. When one of them had 'landed a good thing,' he made it champagne, and invited the rest.

'What a lot of infernal thieves and sweeps they all are!' observed Mullins, referring generally to the statesmen, financiers, and citizens at large of the Guano Free States. Mullins had bribed a Cabinet Minister a little higher than Porter had, and so got a contract for dock, harbour, and granary works, from which pretty pickings were pickable, so much so that Mullins was building a *quinta*, and owned the most expensive china in San José.

'You ought to know,' said Porter, spitting lazily out on the pavement.

'Look at those two bedizened apes!' observed Jack Newbury, the pet failure of the Club, who was guaranteed to waste any fortune, however large, to fail in any financial undertaking, however promising, to lose in any game of chance, to get robbed in any bargain, and to come home without his watch whenever he went on the spree. 'They're specimens of the enemy, I suppose. The tall one's got a lot of decorations, too. Wonder where he got 'em ?'

This referred to our two friends, of whom Macgregor was the one who wore some medals and orders.

'Order of the Black Beetle of Mesopotamia, second class,' murmured Porter.

'Order of the Boot,' said Newbury.

'Stole 'em off a pawnshop, I should think,' suggested Mullins, 'or a theatrical costumier's.'

At this moment a loud scream was heard from the house at the adjacent corner, and a shout of laughter, while a piano descended from the first-floor window with a terrific clang and crash on to the pavement, and a middle-aged man without a hat ran out at the door in the direction of the Club, shouting in English :

'Hi! help! These beggars are sacking my house!'

The three members of the Club ran out, saying, 'Why, it's Shindler!' and found themselves confronted at the outset by Sergeant Lee with his bayonet at the charge, and the two officers with drawn revolvers. Shindler began an indignant protest in halting Spanish, in which the words 'British Consul,' 'Consul Inglez,' frequently occurred, while the other Englishmen backed him up with threats of the awful vengeance which must ensue to those who insulted the divinity that doth hedge a British subject.

Colonel Macgregor said calmly in English : 'Now, can't you tell me quietly what's the matter in some language which you know how to talk ?'— to the considerable astonishment of the members of the Club.

Mr. Shindler explained that some men—soldiers, he presumed, of the Eldorado party—had broken into his house and were plundering it, and that his wife and daughter were in peril and alarm— both British subjects, he added, falling back again into threats about the Consul.

Macgregor said :

'Very well, we'll clear them out. You had better suggest to these friends of yours that the best thing they can do is to go back to their brandy-and-soda and not interfere. They will only make matters worse by making a row.'

' That's so,' said Vane, unable to resist having a dig at Great Britain; 'and mind that we don't care a paper cent for the British Consul, or any other potentate with a lion and unicorn stamped on his——'

' That'll do, Vane; I'm sure these gentlemen will take a hint so delicately put. Now, sir, I am Colonel Macgregor, of the Staff of the United

States of Eldorado, commanding the military force in occupation of this town. Who are you?'

'My name is Shindler—John Shindler—and I have been in business here a matter of twenty years, and am well known to be a——'

'British subject, of course. Well, there's not much mistake about that. Sergeant Lee, go and tell the men to leave Mr. Shindler's house alone, and that I say so. If they won't go, just pitchfork 'em out of window. If they will go, tell them the English gentlemen at the Club will stand them grog and a dollar apiece all round.'

Lee departed at the double.

'Do you come from England, then?' asked Newbury patronizingly of Vane, who happened to be next him, as they stood on the pavement outside Mr. Shindler's house.

'Indeed I do not! I come from a far better place,' was the discouraging reply.

Shortly the three or four men who had invaded the sanctity of a British subject's domicile came clattering out at the front-door, fearful ruffians, with faces covered with powder and blood, and dust and sweat—one or two wounded, and all in a state bordering on sobriety, and carrying Winchester rifles. On seeing Macgregor, they came to attention and ordered their arms. The three Englishmen, whom Mr. Shindler insisted joining in the expense, sent the Club nigger out to them with drinks and dollars on a tray, and the men bowed and smiled with theatrical grace to the sullen and awkward-looking Mullins, Porter, and Newbury, and the scared but relieved Shindler, and amity was restored.

Mr. Shindler thanked Colonel Macgregor pro-

fusely for coming so readily to his relief, and
asked if he and his brother-officer would come in
and take breakfast, which they were about to have
when the unseemly interruption of marauding
soldiery occurred. Macgregor and Vane accepted
with a politeness in which distant courtesy was
intended to hide the famished eagerness of their
acceptance. Macgregor, however, was too old a
soldier to walk into a possible trap with his eyes
shut, so said privily to Sergeant Lee :

'Is it all right inside there?'

'Auvo, Rya ;* there's only some black *charvies*†
and a *pooro chovihani*‡ whooping on her knees
before a silver idol, and a handsome *chi*§ cryin' on
the sofy.'

'Oh, is there? Well, *shoonta tu*,‖ Lee : you take

---

* ' Yes, sir.'   † Children.   ‡ Old witch.
      § Girl.   ‖ Attend.

these sons of a *baulo** with you to Captain Urquiza and tell him 'Teniente Vane and myself are at this house, if required.'

Lee smote his rifle with his left hand, and marched off the four soldiers at a quick pace down towards the Calle 26 Julio.

' Well, gentlemen, if you are ready, perhaps you will come along with me,' said Mr. Shindler, leading the way into his *porte cochère*, which had a marble pavement, pillars, and steps on each side, and led into a wide square *patio*, wholly roofed in with iron trellis-work, on which were trained vines, whose green leaves made a pleasant shade from the sun, which grew hotter every minute as the day went on. In the middle of the *patio* was a well with a white marble mouth and iron lids opening up back to back from a central hinge, and

* Swine.

a wheel, rope and bucket. All round were orange-trees in green tubs. On the right was a door, through which Mr. Shindler led his guests into a room, where they saw the Señora Shindler (a San José lady, the 'old witch' of Sergeant Lee's description, whom he had seen on her knees howling and imprecating to a hideous little silver saint in a shrine), in a white cotton jacket and petticoat, now engaged in scolding at the top of her voice three or four young half-breed servants of both sexes, who were endeavouring to restore order from chaos, and remove the traces of their late visitors. A young lady was standing in the background, with her hair loose and no frock on, of whom our friends had but a glimpse, for both the señora and her daughter fled, banging the door behind them, on the appearance of the gentlemen.

'We're not frightening them, I hope?' said Vane.

'Oh dear no!' said Mr. Shindler; 'it's only that they ain't dressed. I suppose you know that ladies in San José are never dressed till sometime near sunset as a rule. And *then*, O Lor'!'

Mr. Shindler was an iron-gray man, with a shaven, rather crumpled-looking face, small dark eyes, twinkling with something that was partly shrewdness and partly good-nature. He wore a pair of white calico trousers and a black cloth frock-coat, and his manner and speech, though civil, were a trifle vulgar.

'Well,' said he, 'let's go into the dining-room; we'll hurry up the boys and girls a bit—they're shocking lazy; it's something cruel!' And they passed through a door opposite to that by which the ladies had vanished. (All the rooms in these

houses open in and out of one another *en suite*.)
'Now, then, Carlos, Manuela! Concepcion! all
you lazy young idolaters, come and make *desayuno*,
comida, and give me and the señores *aguardiente*,
tres, look alive !'

A grinning half-breed girl of fourteen brought
the *aguardiente*, and Mr. Shindler said :

'Well, here's your health, gentlemen, and you're
welcome ; and I'm sure we're all much obliged to
you for clearing out those—er—valiant warriors of
yours.'

'Not at all,' replied Macgregor, with a pleasant
smile, dropping completely the solemn and pompous
manner he had adopted before the English Club,
with their flannel trousers and brandy-and-soda
and 'side,' which were all red rags both to him and
Vane ; 'I only wish we had arrived sooner, before
the dirty brutes had done any damage. Here's

to ye, sir !' And he threw down the glassful of ardent water at a gulp, and observed: 'That's good.'

'Yerra, I wanted that!' said Vane; 'it's made another man of me.'

'P'raps the other man 'll have another,' said Mr. Shindler, twinkling benevolently, and pleased with his rather ancient joke.

'Sir,' said Vane, 'I'll answer for him—he will. He is proud to make your acquaintance,' he added, draining a second glass of spirits, 'and to drink your health. You're not an Irishman, sir?'

'No, I ain't. I was born in 'Olloway. And some'ow, I'm out here in South America now, with a tidy bit of money and a señora, 'n a 'ouse, in the midst of the pomp and circumstance of glorious war, with shells a-bustin' and shootin' and plunderin' and drummin' and a-trumpetin', and everything to make yer feel 'appy as a bank-'oliday.'

The two officers put their swords and caps in a corner and sat down at their host's invitation, while the servants brought in the breakfast.

'Been in this country long?' asked Mr. Shindler of Macgregor. 'I mean, in any of 'em? I count Eldorado and Guano and Piguador and the rest as all the same sort of thing, with no offence to you.'

'Mercy, no! We would be as happy to lend our swords to one State as to the other, but we are bound in honour to the one with which we have contracted. In answer to your question, both Vane, myself, and Captain Doherty, of our ship, entered the service of the Estados Unidos of Eldorado at the outbreak of the present war. We were all acquainted with Spanish, and had some previous experience of soldiering, in various ways; and we

all started with the treasure-chest nearly empty,
but we are reforming that indifferently now—aren't
we, Pat?'

'We are indeed. Ah, sir, you ought to ask
Colonel Macgregor to tell you some of his adven-
tures! He's been through more in fifteen years
than many a British Field-Marshal has in fifty.'

'Oh, we'll get him to talk after breakfast, I
hope!'

'I shall be glad to give an account of myself,'
said Macgregor. 'Not that I've anything to boast
of, but because I think a Highland gentleman
ought to say who he is and where he comes from,
so that any society he may be in may know that
they are not entertaining a d——d snob or thief,
or person of no kin.'

'So you're a Scotchman, are you? I thought
so.'

'Surr! I am a Highlander, who is not the same thing as what you call a Scotchman. Glasgow tradesmen and Edinburgh writers are Scotchmen, and there are Scotch gentlemen in the Lothians and towards the Border, no doubt. I would not say that there are not.'

'But,' said Vane, 'the old original inhabitants of Scotland, who were there before the Romans or the English, or anyone else except the hills and the water, came from Ireland. And that's the crowd Colonel Macgregor belongs to. I'm a Sligo man meself.'

'I see,' said Mr. Shindler, thinking to himself: 'Touchy beggars, gassing about their blessed ancestry and all! Mustn't offend them, especially as they're in command of two or three hundred thieves with repeating rifles.'

'Ah!' he said aloud, 'here are the ladies.'

· The two officers sprang to their feet, as the Señora Shindler (born of the distinguished family of Ximio y Pelagatos) and her daughter entered. The ladies curtseyed, and the gentlemen bowed deeply.

Mrs. Shindler (to be more prosaic) was a fat woman whose beauty had left her some ten or fifteen years ago, though she was not old as far as actual time reckons age, and she was firmly persuaded that she was quite beautiful still, and did everything in her power to propagate that illusion. But she required much preparation before encountering publicity, and little Concepcion and Carlos had far from agreeable quarters and halves of hours ministering to the necessities of her toilet, as Mrs. Shindler had a habit of flying into shrieking tempers and whacking her attendants on the head with a hair-brush or boot or anything con-

5

venient when the face she watched in the mirror failed to produce the perfect illusion, even on herself, which she expected others to find in it. Nevertheless, though usually unkempt and in untidy wrappers all day, until after the afternoon sleep, the presence of two gentlemen—two officers (it did not the least matter whether they were the enemy or not; they were in any case men, and would admire her)—on this particular day, had actually stimulated her into getting dressed by about twelve, when the breakfast was served, nearly an hour later than its usual time. Her waist was compressed ('squashed in,' old John Shindler called it; but he was not a refined stylist) as much as anything short of hydraulic pressure could compress it; her face and hands had been washed—really washed—with soap and water, and beautifully coloured; her hair was done with all the

elaboration the fashion allowed, and was of a
glossy black like the surface of hard coal, and had
a yellow rose in it on one side; her nails were
highly polished, and dyed deep pink; her dress
was in the latest European fashion, though more
gay in colouring, as is usual in this warm land,
where the very birds dress in gorgeous colours.
She was not ridiculously fat or ugly, not at all.
She was an originally charming woman on whom
time had rapidly told, as is usual with her race
and climate. It need hardly be added that she
was ignorant as dirt, superstitious, lazy, passionate-
tempered, and deadly jealous of her daughter, who
was in all the mature beauty of nineteen.

Miss Shindler was a slender girl of about five
feet one, with a perfect figure—a kind of dark-
haired beauty, which in some manner suggested
a feline element—eyes half shy, half sly, hands

and feet which were a perpetual delight (and she knew it), and a lithe facility of movement which again shadowed forth the cat-idea. Her eyes were a fine amber brown, and there was just the faintest black shadowing of down at the corners of her mouth, fading towards the middle of the upper lip. She was dressed in black and yellow lace, and wore little scarlet flowers in each ear instead of earrings. Her complexion was rich and delicate, rose and tawny, and her whole seductive person was *miching mallecho*—it meant mischief.

There are grades as well as styles of beauty in womankind, which may be classified as rising from the woman who is said to sometimes look 'rather pretty' in a favourable costume and light, and at a certain distance, the lower limit, to the indisputable, victorious loveliness which compels acknowledgment, in any costume, in any light, in

any attitude, or under any external variation whatever, the higher limit.   Miss or Señorita Mary
Carmen Juanita Josefina Shindler belonged, if not
to that last supreme class, to one approximate to
it.   Cressida was not Helen, though Troilus, the
guileless young gentleman, as well as Agamemnon,
the experienced man-leader and war-lord, and
Diomedes, the bold wooer, found much to admire
in her, as well as Menelaus (who, by the way, was
in the best position to make comparisons between
her and Helen).

The worst thing that Miss Shindler's mother in
her worst temper could say of her daughter was
that she had a face fit to put on the lid of a
chocolate-box.

And they sat down to *puchéro*.

A peculiarity of Miss Shindler was that, though
speaking Spanish like her mother—that is, in the

way those who may be called the upper classes spoke it—she spoke English like her father, pronouncing it with a curious foreign caricature of his Cockney accent, arbitrary grammar, and sometimes unrefined expressions. She had very few Englishmen to speak to in San José society, and they, too, were often slangy and vulgar, so that she had no steady and permanent standard to compare with and regulate by except her father. She soon noticed, of course, that Macgregor and Vane spoke differently, but put it down to variety in dialect, such as usually obtains in the different ethnographical divisions of any large State, in which she was, of course, partially right. The Señora spoke broken English only.

'Señor Coronel,' said the young lady, 'you keeked up an 'orrible row this morning. It put me off my sleep, something c—r—uel.'

'I am sure I regret it, señorita, but I am afraid you began. All we required was a contribution, which we would willingly have just accepted peaceably, when your brave forces opened fire on us.'

'Oh, don't mix me op with that lot; I'm English!'

'Ye look it,' said Vane; 'and if we'd known it would prolong one of your beautiful dreams, señorita, we'd have used noiseless powder.'

'My gel don't talk English so bad for one who's never been in England in her life,' said Mr. Shindler; 'but she'll have an opportunity of pickin' up a bit more exper'ence soon. I've made my pile, as the Yankees say, in this bloomin' country, and I can see it's going into bankruptcy as fast as it knows how, and I'm off. We're all off, mar and Mary and me, next boat. When I see this war was comin' off, I reelized all my s'curities and put 'em in the bank here, so I've only got to draw a cheque for the lot and post it to a London bank. I shall 'ave a nice little 'ouse out 'Ampstead way, and keep a trap for Mary and mar, and we'll all drive over of a Sunday to the Welsh 'Arp.'

'Aha!' said Señora Shindler, with an eager gesture, and a sort of high nasal voice, easily developing into a scolding scream or a tearful whoop. 'Nobeel'ty, dey go dere? No. Aha! Vere nobeel'ty go, I go. I am daughter of President of Guano; I religious, I aristocratic. I g—o—o—o—od!' (working up to a scream). 'You not know how good I am. An' I marree dat mahn. Ah! bah!' and she pointed a derisive, malevolent finger at the unfortunate Shindler, who, however, only grinned indifferently and winked. It had in the course of years vaguely dawned on his wife that John Shindler was not a member of the highest English aristocracy, and she was not one to veil her disappointments, or wrongs, or merits, real or imaginary, where she thought sympathy might be obtained by unveiling them.

Macgregor interposed with something approaching tact, by saying :

' May I ask which bank you placed your property in, Mr. Shindler ? Was it by any chance the Banco Nacional ?'

' Yes, that's it ?'

' Then it's extremely probable that it is on board the *Infierno* at the present moment,' replied Macgregor grimly, 'as every kind of available security, coupon payable to bearer, convairtible or inconvairtible paper, bill of exchange, cash, gold or silver plate, or other valuable, found in that bank was going in carts under escort down to the boats from an early hour this f'r'noon.'

'No, I say, are you sure of that?'

'I gave the orders to have it done.'

'Then the bank's no good?'

'*As* a bank, it is ineffectual by this time. But it will be very useful to quarter some of the men in.'

'My prop'ty was the amount to the credit of my account. The bank was bound to pay that amount to my cheque on due notice, and I'd given the notice. Now all the bank's assets is on board your infernal gunboat, what am I to do? What might you be going to do with the swag, as, in a manner of speaking, you might call it now you've landed it, or rather shipped it?'

'Speaking only as an instrument under the orders of higher powers, and not as one in their secrets, but rather as one with a pretty considerable experience of their interesting peculiarities, I would deem it probable that a large proportion will be divided according to rank and seniority among the ship's company. That Captain Doherty will hand over the balance (if any) to the Government at Eldorado, and to avoid mistakes or forgetfulness on the part of that Government, will effect the division of prize-money furrst, and transmit to the Government later.'

Mr. Shindler arose from his seat and quickly sat down again, swallowed a glass of wine, and said :

'Do you mean to tell me that your beastly Government is going to quietly pocket my—— Oh, I say, look here, Colonel, you're a gentleman, you are, and a good feller ! Yere am I with a wife and child, and nothing but the 'ome we live in, and our close and a few nicknacks, if I can't get my money. 'Oo's goin' to buy my 'ouse either, times like these ? What am I to do ? Tell me that.'

'Ye ask hard questions, Mr. Shindler.'

Vane had been exchanging amiable trivialities with the mother and daughter, the former of whom hardly understood, while the latter paid no attention to her father's conversation, until the last sentence or two, which caught both her ear and Vane's. Miss Shindler asked Vane what it all meant, and he told her in English. She replied to him in a low voice in the same language, that they had better conceal it as long as possible from her mother, who would probably have a fit and yell and break things. In the meantime she looked at Vane, who sat alongside her, and said :

'You will make it all right, Señor 'Teniente. Yes ?'

Vane looked at her, surrendered at discretion, and said :

' All right, my dear; I'll see what I can do, you may be sure. We'll work it.'

Mary Carmen Juanita Josefina pressed his hand gently under the table, and looked at him again, and poor Pat Vane felt he could sell his soul for her—only, he meditated, no one would take his soul at prairie value, or any other price. Well, well, Mary Carmen had known pretty well how to make love since she was eleven, and now she was in her twentieth year, so there was not much chance for a *comparative* neophyte like Vane, who, although, of course, much older than Miss Shindler, had a naturally boyish temperament, was very susceptible to the seductiveness of fair femininity in general, but had, among passing experiences, not yet had the one experience which divides a man's life into before and after he loved such an one.

But now Mary Shindler was such an one. Pat

Vane drank a mouthful of wine (he had had a good many mouthfuls), and said to his comrade :

'Mac, why shouldn't Mr. Shindler and the señora and señorita come on board, and be taken to Eldorado? They would find a ship there for Europe soon, and make a claim on the Government for their property. We can't say their passage isn't paid, any way.'

'I see no objection to that course, but I would obsairve that making a claim on the Government of Eldorado is one thing, and obtaining what you claim from them is another. I am thinking that it would not be an easy matter. It is not logical to bribe a man with a hundred pounds to give you back a thousand which he has control over. And without bribes the wheels of justice grind slowly in Eldorado. And if you make use of the British Consul and gunboat machinery, they have to be

convinced, in the furrst instance, that the Eldorado
Government reelly have possession of your property, of which it would be difficult to obtain proof.
Oh, it would be a fairly uphill chob! It would
that.' And Colonel Macgregor placidly swallowed
some wine, and added: 'That's good stuff, sir.'

'Then, what the devil *am* I to do?' said Mr.
Shindler, driven desperate by the long, grim,
swarthy Highlander's deliberate observations and
apparent absolute indifference to what became of
his—John Shindler's—property.

'We might sacrifice the Government's share,'
suggested Vane, 'and hand it over to Mr. Shindler.
What do you say, Mac?'

'We might. Or we might deduct from the
Government's share an amount equal to the
amount entrusted by Mr. Shindler to the Banco
Nacional. There would be a kind of equity in that.'

'Mike Doherty's not specially disposed to go out of his way to do favours for the English, it is true; but it is the State, rather than the individual, he's opposed to.'

'Ay. Moreover, Mr. Shindler has suffered by no fault of his own, and has been most polite to us.'

'Well, look 'ere now, gentlemen,' said Mr. Shindler, with eager hope reviving; 'I'm a man who understands business, y' know, and I'll only say this, that I 'ope you and the gentlemen on board the *Inferno* won't let any reasonable little commission stand in your way—say five or six— or well, there, I'd go as far as seven and a 'arf on the total recovered.'

'Surr!' said Macgregor sternly, 'we may take our share of the spoil of war fairly won by the sword; we may keep it or, if it pleases us, we may fling it into the ocean in ducks and drakes; but we're not mere tradesmen.'

'Well, I beg pardon, I'm sure; but I thought,' Shindler added with a plausible and disarming grin—'thought perhaps you might look on it as ransom for turning your chaps out of this house— spoil of war, as you say. Only just by way of a joke, y' know.'

'That,' replied Macgregor, appeased, 'alters the matter, and places it on a footing on which a soldier and a gentleman can treat. Surr, in that sense, I accept your tairms, and we will call it ten per centum on the tottal recovered. Here's your health. Beso los manos señora y señorita.'

And as he glanced *à la dérobée* at Vane, something resembling a wink floated or flashed across the dry gravity of Colonel Macgregor's countenance.

By this time the señora, by eager cross-examina-
tion of her daughter, had arrived at a conception
of her own of the matter under discussion, and
broke out into loud lamentation and scolding, in
which, as usual, her husband's shortcomings, and
her own merits and ancestry, formed the theme.

'Ah! We ruined! Dat mahn! Look at eem!
Euh-h! Ee bizniss mahn? No! Ee gentlemahn? No! Ah, vy I leaf my fammillee? My
fammillee, firstest in Guano. Ximio y Pelagatos
ce gentlemahn! An' you, vy you come 'ere?
You say you caballeros y officiales del Eldorado.
No! You tief! English tief! Ah!'

Mr. Shindler said:

'Will you hold your silly jabbering tongue?
You know nothing at all about the matter. These
gentlemen are doing their best to arrange for the
recovery of my property, and if it 'adn't a-bin for

them, this 'ouse we're sitting in would have been gutted as clean as burglary, and most likely set afire as well. They are kind enough to take us off in their ship, too, to Eldorado, where we can get a steamer to England, and leave this beastly country be'ind us for good.'

' I go to Eldorado ? No; nevare ! I stay wid my fammillee.'

' Then you bloomin' well *can* stay, that's all ! Mary, tell your mother to pack her things up, and see that she does it, and not to make more fool of herself than she can help.' And Miss Shindler, with a last glance at Vane and a bow to Macgregor, persuaded her mother to leave the room. Mr. Shindler gave a sigh of relief, and said : ' Don't either of you chaps ever marry a full-bred lady of the firstest family in San José. 'Elp yourself to *aguardiente*, Colonel, and shove the bottle round.

What'd you and me give for a good Scotch cold now, eh, at the Palmerston or Winchester 'Ouse ?'

'I say, Mac, do you know Whelan's in Lower Abbey Street ? That was the place for whisky. I've not been in it now for fifteen years.'

'Man, there's only one kind of whisky. Hullo ! what's that ?'

'That' was the distinct sound of a cannon shot, and not very far off.

The two officers jumped up and buckled on their swords. In a minute or two Sergeant Lee arrived, announcing that he wished to see Colonel Macgregor privately. The Colonel went out to see him, and when he returned said :

'Pat, it seems we did not seize the telegraph soon enough. There's a force with artillery been sent up by rail from Perique to attack us. They were seen by Doherty some miles off, and a party

was sent to pull up the rails as far outside as they
had time to go. Lieutenant von Kries drove an
engine himself out to meet them, and halted, put
dynamite under the rails with a time fuse, reversed
and came back on the engine into the town.
Doherty fired that gun at their train as it halted,
but the range was bad. They are advancing by
way of the hills on the south side of the town. As
soon as they've got their guns into position they'll
probably shell the town to drive us out. Most of
the men are on board, and we've to be away now.
Lee has a small escort, because the scattered
Guano men we defeated this morning are taking
up courage again, and beginning to show in groups
in the town.'

' Can't we hold the place?'

' Not the shadow of a chance. We shall be commanded by their artillery, and they will be almost

out of range of the ship. Besides, the *Almirante McCarthy* may be coming too. She may have been within reach of Perique, and got signalled somewhere along the shore.—Now, Mr. Shindler, fetch your womenkind. Never mind luggage. There's not a moment to lose. The house will be tumbling about your ears soon.'

Mr. Shindler ran away, and soon loud expostulations and screamings betokened the señora's unwillingness to leave before she had made up her mind to the proper head-dress, or something equally important. In the meantime Macgregor and Vane went out to the Plaza, where Sergeant Lee had got about ten files of men extended at four paces, with the house in their rear, with loaded rifles. On the other side of the Plaza, from the Calle 26 Julio, debouched a number of Guano natives, reunited stragglers from the military force and miscellaneous unmilitary loafers with rifles, and these promptly opened fire, taking cover behind the orange-trees and marble benches. Lee's men lay down and fired rapid volleys by Colonel Macgregor's orders, and then charged the opposite force with the bayonet, sending them down the Calle 26 Julio helter-skelter.

'This is a good beginning,' remarked Colonel Macgregor.

'There's dozens of those *baulos* to get through betwixt us and the *lun-pawni*,'* observed Lee, shoving in fresh cartridges with his thumb. 'They're picking up a bit now.'

'We'll sort them to rights,' observed Macgregor, placidly getting out his revolver and loosening his sword.

'We can go through them as easy as lyin',' said

---

* Salt-water.

Vane; 'but it will be the least bit awkward getting two ladies down there.'

'They'll just have to kilt up their coats and do a steady double, taking advantage of the trees in the *calle*. They can have the rifles and pouches of the first two men dropped on either side.'

'My bonnie boy, when did ye ever see a Spanish woman who could double fifty yards? And as to cover, you'd have to tell off a man to each to tell 'em what cover is, and get 'em to leave it when they've found out.'

'Well, they may just do what they blame please. I am doing the best I can for them, and I can't stay here until those sons of Shaitan get seeing us, and drop shells in. It would be wasting the men's lives (not that they're worth much) for nothing, and risk not getting away with the loot, which *is* worth much.'

Here Mr. Shindler and the two ladies appeared, carrying as much jewellery as could be packed into hand-bags.

' Now, sir,' said Macgregor, ' you and the ladies must conform to our movements, and had better keep in the immediate rear. No—not in a clump, clinging to one another like that ! Extend, ye daft women, extend ! Ye don't want to make a target of yourselves ! Miss Shindler, go in the rear of Mr. Vane on the right. Mr. Shindler, go in rear of Sergeant Lee on the left. The señora can keep behind me, in the centre. Now conform to the movement of the section. Section, advance ! Half-left-turn ! Right shoulders up ! Double ! Halt ! Lie down ! Fire volleys by alternate half-sections beginning from the right !'

The movement had brought them across the top of the Calle 26 Julio, in which some opposition was found. The feelings of the unhappy Shindler family may be imagined. Miss Shindler lay down beside Vane in the white dust, regardless of her really expensive and becoming costume, and displayed much more courage than might have been expected, though she winced every time she heard the shrill little 'feee-ew!' of a bullet not far off, followed perhaps by the smash of a window-pane in the rear. When one of the men was hit, the sight of blood made her turn rather sick, and Vane, observing her face, said :

'Now for the sake of our Blessed Lady, my dear, don't faint! You'll have to double again in half a minute. Here, take a drop of this !'

And he handed her a glass flask with which he had replaced his smashed water-bottle, and she drank. It was *aguardiente*. Then she said :

'I am better now. I am not afraid.'

'And I don't believe you are, then!'

'Rise! Advance! Double!' sang out Macgregor.

When they halted and lay down again, this time half-way down the street, where another street crossed it at right angles, the girl said breathlessly to Vane:

'Do you think we shall ever get to your ship?'

'Oh, divil doubt us! That is, if the enemy are not reinforced. They know we gave 'em a good hammering this morning, and all the prestige is on our side. But they're obstinate young men, too.'

'Ah, listen! What is that, Señor Vane?' she exclaimed, getting up on her knees in her excitement to point. 'Those men, they are cötting off, they are ronning away! Ah, *los chanchos!*'*

* I fear Miss Shindler really used another expression.

Vane jumped to his feet.

'Great Cæsar, you are right! Mike Doherty's landed himself with a party and taken 'em in flank.' And he gave an Irish yell of triumph and defiance. Colonel Macgregor, with his usual coolness, and a streaming wound on the side of the face, said :

'Rise! Fix bayonets! On the centre close! Quick march! Double! Prepare to charge! Charge!' And he and Vane went running on in front, and leaping over the obstacles encumbering the street, which the enemy had lugged out of the houses for cover, with the men shouting behind, until, for the second time, their enemy had been cleared out of their position, while Doherty's men were 'giving them pepper' from the flank as they fled.

'There, señorita,' said Vane, 'you've been in an

action in the ranks. And it's not many young ladies can say that.'

Here Captain Doherty came up and said :

' What in the world have you boys been doing ? Do you know there's not a minute to lose ? There, look at that now !' he added, as a shell burst with a bright dazzling flame and a loud report in the Plaza della Independencia. Colonel Macgregor went to Doherty, and reported briefly all that had occurred ; and Doherty, after bowing to the Shindlers, said :

' Well, just come on board, all of you, and let's get under way, or the ladies will have to figure in a naval action as well as a land one. We can discuss all the rest later on. Form up now, never mind numbering — look alive ! Fours ! Right ! Left wheel ! Double—march !'

The señora had never had so much ' doubling '

in her life. She had no breath to talk about her
'fammillee,' and was dragged along by Mr.
Shindler on one side, and Sergeant Lee on the
other. She didn't mind the bloodshed a bit, she
had seen too many bull-fights for that, but she
hated running.

Meanwhile, the enemy approaching on the hills
began to drop shells more frequently, in a casual
way, in hopes of swamping the boats, which were
barely in range. Then the ship began to fire
shells at the hill-top battery, but they fell short.

The upshot was that Vane and Macgregor and
the Shindler family all got safely on board, and
the *Infierno y Tomasito* started for Eldorado with
a quantity of valuables and money on board which
would have been no despicable prize even to good
Sir Francis Drake.

CHAPTER II.

HOW MR. HARRY LONG TRIED A LITTLE POACHING, AND CAUGHT A LITTLE POACHER.

ONE summer afternoon five or six years after the events of the first chapter, a young man came down to Shervil, a station somewhere between Salisbury and Exeter, where a groom and a dog-cart awaited him. He was a fine, tall fellow, about two-and-twenty, not as heavy and robust yet as he would be in a few years' time, yet active and healthy, with a handsome fair face and blue eyes, and a rather more refined expression than is usual among young gentlemen of England, whose gods are athletes and their devils examiners. He bestowed a donation on the porter who carried his portmanteau, bag, ulster, and tennis-racquet in brown canvas case to the dogcart with a good-natured greeting, as if he had come back to old friends, as, indeed, he had; and as he got up and drove away from the station, there were several who touched their caps to him, from the station-master downwards.

This young man had come 'down' for his second Long Vacation from Cambridge, a period at which undergraduate life may be said to be at the summit of its glory, having left 'freshness' well behind, and having as yet the Tripos a good long way ahead. He was a tolerably happy young man, having a comfortable allowance, good rooms in the Old Court, furnished and decorated according to his tastes, a pleasant temper, plenty of friends, no embarrassing entanglements either in connection with money or the other sex, and an opinion of himself and his attainments which was generally highly favourable, and had not yet been at all seriously upset by events. There is usually a tide in the affairs of moderately conceited, rather clever young men which sooner or later overwhelms them with the awful conviction that they have been making fools of themselves, but young Mr. Harry Long had not yet been overtaken by it.

He was full of all the modern ideas, books, and modes of thought, had interested himself in æsthetics, politics, philanthropy, misanthropy, poetry, pessimism, peacocks' feathers, and Parisian novels; spoke at the Union; talked with great earnestness and eloquence to sympathetic friends, as they tramped together in the afternoon along the Trumpington Road to do the 'Granchester Grind,' about everything in the world; and in a

general way was ready to send in tenders and
specifications for completely recasting the universe
on a new and improved plan. He was impatient
of old formalities, of proverbial sayings, of all
obvious and commonplace things. Being the only
son of an old country squire, Sir William Long of
Lowcliff, of iron-fast Tory principles, it is only
natural that his political views, as they came out
at the Union, Magpie and Stump, and elsewhere,
should vary from advanced Radicalism to Home
Rule.

The drive from Shervil Station to Lowcliff was
some five miles along a road which skirted a
beautiful winding wooded valley, in the bottom of
which a river ran, which enlarged to a creek
navigable for small boats further down, forming
an inner portion of Starmouth Bay. The whole
country hereabouts is hilly, and the little gray

slatey town of Starmouth itself looks as if it had been piled up the side of a hill from the shore, or been arrested in the act of tumbling down into the sea, many centuries ago. And everywhere you walk or drive, steep lanes and green valleys are your portion. You are also in perpetual doubt as to whether you are in Dorset or Devon, as the counties overlap, or intersect in irregular jags, in a surprising way.

But from where young Harry Long and his groom were driving homewards, there were only far-off gray glimpses of the Channel and projecting reddish headlands, and the town of Starmouth was not visible at all. They passed through the village of Redmore, an assemblage of white stone cottages with thatched roofs, standing beside the steep slope of a narrow curving road, where children and fowls ran and tumbled and shrieked and crowed, doing their best to get entangled in the wheels of the dogcart, and women stood at the doors in sun-bonnets, and gazed vaguely at the smart convey-ance, some perhaps curtseying. After passing the Dog Inn, at the extreme end of Redmore, and the bottom of the dip of the road, they drove uphill again, and passed a lonely small thatched cottage, not in particularly good repair, giving somehow the impression that the inside would be dirty, though the outside was charming, and had ivy and a yellow-flowered creeper growing in the little garden in front, between it and the road. In the open doorway of this cottage sat, on a low stool, an ancient woman with sharp, dark eyes, and a bright red-and-yellow kerchief round her neck. It may be added that she was smoking a short clay pipe of a dark polished mouse-colour. Near her stood a girl of twenty or so, who had risen from picking some flowers in order to look at Harry Long, who was certainly worth looking at, especially by a girl who had never seen him before. And this girl was wonderfully pretty. She had the dark, keen eyes of the old woman, a sunburnt, sallow complexion, black hair, arranged more or less in the prevailing fashion, but rather untidy, a perfectly proportioned body, rather above the average height, clad in an old brown frock, such as might once have belonged to some lady who had given it to her maid, who had handed it on in course of time to this young person. As the road was uphill, Harry drove slowly, and had a good look at her. And she had a good look at him. When they were out of sight and hearing, Harry said to the groom:

'I don't remember ever seeing those people there before. Are they Irish, or what?'

'No, sir, gipsy. Family of the name of Lee. The man Lee, the old woman's son, was brought here by way of a manservant by the gentleman who's taken Crowhill.'

'Crowhill taken too, eh? Well?'

'Yes, sir. And this man Lee, he brought his old witch of a mother and daughter here, and found that place empty and put 'em in. Used to trampin' the roads, and sleepin' in 'edges, they are, I expecs. Regular poachers, all the lot. Shouldn't wonder if that was some of our game we smelt there cooking.'

'Ah, well, I don't suppose we shall miss it much!'

'Sir William's terrible put out about it. None of the keepers can't catch this chap at it. Sharp hands, they gipsies, at takin' what ain't theirn.'

'So are kings and capitalists, Rogers; but no

matter. Don't let me corrupt a good Conservative like you. Who is it, then, that has taken Crowhill? I thought that it was going to be handed over to ghosts in perpetuity.'

Crowhill was a tall old brick house with tiled gables, attic windows, and ivy-clad chimneys, on a windy eminence on the other side of the valley, lonely-looking, with one or two tall weather-beaten fir-trees standing close to it, black against the western sky, and farther away, in the field near the house, a group of high elms with graceful green cascades of foliage, in whose dizziest heights rooks built and circled cawing.

Below the house, down the slope of the valley, an oak and hazel copse descended to the river, where was a private wooden landing-place for boats, hidden by trees, unless one were actually standing on it. The old house had a fair amount of land,

partly fields, and partly wood and copse, where
hares and rabbits had their abode, to say nothing
of hedgehogs and wood-pigeons, and was roomy,
picturesque, and cosy, though exposed to south-
westerly weather when ' depressions' arrived in the
Channel. Still, it had been vacant for years, and
was to be had at a price far below its apparent
value, simply and solely because the last occupant,
an elderly clergyman of peculiar habits—a bachelor
possessing considerable private means—had elected
to leave this world in an original instead of a
commonplace manner. Not content with dying in
bed of natural decay, accelerated by chill, like a
respectable ordinary old gentleman, he had hung
himself with strong twine to a hook in the larder
between a spare-rib of pork and a fillet of veal; and
in consequence of this tenants were very shy of the
place, and no servants belonging to the neighbour-

hood would have taken situations there, had the house been occupied, as will be readily understood.

'It's a gentleman and lady of the name of Vane,' replied Rogers. 'He's quite a stranger in these parts—come from America, they tell me; but quite the gentleman. Seems to have a middlin' lot of money, and the lady is foreign, but a very 'ansome lady. Mr. Vane 'e looks like an army gentleman; 'e 'as a little cutter yacht, but 'e don't keep no 'osses nor no family.'

'Does anybody know them?'

'Well, sir, we've called on 'em, and so 'as some of the other gentry, and 'aven't no fault to find, except that they're both Roman Catholics. But they're strong Kinservatives, and that's the great thing.'

'Of course it is.'

'We're givin' a garden-party to-morrow, sir, it being only put off till you come back, and you'll see 'em there, I expect.'

'I see. All right.'

And they drove on till Lowcliff, the residence of Sir William Long, was reached, an old country house nestling in the side of the wooded valley, with gables and a tiled roof, and delightful variations in the levels of the different rooms, but covered externally with gray plaster by some tasteless improver of a generation or two gone by.

Here Harry received a good old English welcome, which grated a little on his new refinement as a little too *bruyant*, from his father, an iron-gray old man, a J.P. of course, and a pillar of the constitution, a loyal, stern, narrow-minded, honourable gentleman, a little inconsistent at times, and possessing much kindness of heart. He was at an early stage of his life in the army, when by the unexpected death of a brother he suddenly came in for the baronetcy and the estate of Lowcliff. He had all the views on life of a country gentleman of the old school, and looked on hunting and shooting as serious things, and on poachers and persons who shot foxes as inferior only in criminality to Socialists. Lady Long was an excellent old lady, stout, without form and very void. There was one other child— a girl, a year younger than Harry, with fair light-brown crisp hair, light-blue eyes, large in the iris and small in the pupil, a pointed chin, a rather aquiline nose—altogether of a charming appearance which no map-like analysis can convey, over whose birth a star had danced, as in the case of Beatrice, and they called her Elizabeth, a name in which Sir William's historic tastes and Lady Long's fondness for Jane Austen's novels happily concurred. They both agreed in disliking new-fangled ' pretty ' names of the Ethel, Olga, Gladys, Muriel class, so they christened her Elizabeth, which she thought bad, and called her Bessie, which she thought worse. Nevertheless she bore up, consoling herself with the reflection that she had not been called Louisa, Harriet, or Ann, as she might easily have been— ' what with English history and Jane Austen,' as she said, ' hovering like malignant fairies over one's cradle. I should like Jane Austen very much if mother did not point out her merits so forcibly, and I could tolerate history if father didn't look on it as a kind of trumpet to announce the greatness of England with and proclaim the Protestant Succession.'

At dinner that evening they asked Harry questions about Cambridge—the questions a young man's relations always do ask. Sir William asked

how many undergraduates there were now at
Trinity, what time he had left in the morning,
and how the connection of trains had been made
(thereby involving his son quite needlessly in an
obligatory series of fictions to cover the fact that
he left Cambridge the day before and spent the
night in town), and proceeded to make a few
remarks about sliding-seats, which betrayed an
imperfect grasp of the subject, though Harry,
whose rowing was mainly confined to paddling up
the Freshman's river in a pair, and taking shandy-
gaff at the Red Lion of Granchester, could forgive him that. Harry rather sniffed at the earnest
rowing man, and classified him (quite unfairly)
with vulgar dissipation, paltry ambitions, a
'General' postponed to the utmost limits of
University tolerance, and an *ægrotat* in the Botany
Special. (The latter is the typical destiny scorn-

fully predicted for Cambridge men of low intellectual attainment by their more gifted com-
panions.)

Lady Long asked him how long his holidays
would last, on which Sir William jocularly interposed:

'Mustn't call them holidays now, y' know.'

While Harry replied:

'Oh, till October, as usual! I don't the least
mind your calling the Long the holidays, or the
tomatoes, if you like. I think we have gone
through that delectable little joke, in this family,
every time I have come down, with regularity
and precision. Don't you think you could get
up a new set of *facetiæ* against the Christmas
Vac?'

'Well, I don't know, my boy, we'll try,' replied
Sir William good-humouredly; 'but our wits are

not kept in such a high state of polish as all that. You must put up with us as you find us.'

This had the exasperating effect of making Harry feel that he was looked on as pert and conceited, and yet too well liked and too young to be thoroughly snubbed. He was convinced that in any mental capacity or attainment he was far superior to his parents, and yet, just because they were his parents and some trivial thirty years or so older than he was, they failed to recognise his claim to any such superiority, and continued to give him advice and information on matters most of which he felt he understood far better than they did. This kind of treatment is liable to make a gifted youth impatient at times.

Bessie asked if there had been many people and much going on that May term, and Harry gave suitable descriptions.

Then Sir William said:

'Have they told you what that fellow Herrick has been doing?'

'That fellow Herrick' was the vicar of the parish.

'No, I don't think so. What has he been doing?'

'Why, he's put up a crucifix on the Communion-table, and two candles.'

'Not a crucifix, dear—a cross,' corrected Lady Long.

'Oh!' replied Harry, with carefully marked in-difference.

'I told him pretty plainly it was a direct encouragement to idolatry.'

'But if people feel "so dispoged," why shouldn't they worship idols? I know a man who has col-lected some lovely idols from some of the Pacific islands, or somewhere, and has arranged them in his keeping-room, and burns a pastille to the most appalling of them occasionally, when he feels an access of devotion coming over him. He says it is more original than chapel, and less irreverent.'

' Harry! How can you say such things?' said his mother.

Bessie smiled quietly to herself. She knew who the idolater was, and was rather fond of him.

' Surely,' continued Lady Long, ' we are distinctly forbidden to worship idols?'

' Of course,' said Harry ; ' but there is the charm. That is the only reason probably why the primitive Hebrew tribes were so fond of lapsing into different forms of it. What would otherwise have been an uninteresting, and occasionally uncomfortable, waste of time, destined to become obsolete with advancing intelligence and civilization, was perpetuated into a fascinating sin, traces of which last even to this day, as has just been pointed out, simply because of a tactless prohibition accompanied by threats. Instead of saying, "You mustn't, because it's wicked," you should say, 'Well, if I were you, I'd drop it, because it's rather feeble and cramps your ideas," if you want people to leave off doing a thing.'

'I must say you do pick up extraordinary ideas at Cambridge!' said Lady Long.

'Well, isn't that what I'm there for? If I was only required and expected to accumulate ordinary ideas, it would have been simpler for me to have stopped here, wouldn't it?'

'Oh, don't argue, dear! it makes my head ache.'

'No, don't let us argue, especially at dinner. But tell me, you remember J. R. Shaw, that I coach with sometimes? You saw him, you know, when you were up at the Lent races.'

'Oh yes! I remember him quite well. Very nice, isn't he?'

'Well, he's not considered nasty as a rule.'

'A gentlemanly, civil young fellow,' said Sir William; 'gave us doosid good claret, too.'

Bessie said nothing, but searched for crumbs, which she made into pills.

'Well, do you mind my asking him down here for a week or two?'

'Certainly not, my boy,' said Sir William; 'ask him by all means. Tell him not to coach you into a prig.'

'We shall be very glad to see him, I'm sure,' said Lady Long.

'Are you going to do some work, then?' said Bessie.

'Oh, I shall read a little—not very much—just enough to chasten one's style. I gather from Rogers that you have some new neighbours at Crowhill?'

'Oh yes!' replied Lady Long, delighted to escape from the uphill effort of talking about things and principles to the easy level of talking about people; 'and they seem very nice indeed. I think Mr. Vane has been at one time in some foreign service, and he has that appearance, rather. He is very civil and agreeable, and she is rather pretty, with something a little foreign and rather taking about her.'

' She dresses like an American,' said Bessie.

'Then she must dress very well,' replied her brother.

'They are Roman Catholics,' said Sir William; 'but they seem to be decent sort of people.'

'I suppose that means they have subscribed to the Conservative Association?'

'That's just what it does mean, my boy,' replied Sir William, chuckling; 'and come down pretty handsome, too.'

'And Mrs. Vane sang and played the guitar at a Primrose League entertainment,' added Bessie.

'I see. Well, of course, the Conservatives are the elect—if not always the elected.'

'But I do wish to goodness,' pursued Sir William, 'that they wouldn't keep a gipsy man about the place, or, if they did, that they would give him something more to do. The way he poaches is something awful. Nothing is safe from him. I gather that he keeps a family entirely on it, and he is more than a match for any keepers about here. He seems to know all their tricks, and a good many more besides. I used to think that Nobbs must connive, but I am sure now that such is not the case.   Once we put up one or two alarm spring-guns—you know, the ones you screw on a tree, and have a wire stretched across the pathway tightly from the trigger; and then the beggar runs against it in the dark, and off it goes, bang!'

'But isn't that rather dangerous?' interposed Lady Long.

'No, no; dangerous, no!   It's only an explosion of a charge of powder, for the noise to attract Nobbs's attention, and tell him there's someone in the copse.   The law, bless its old grandmotherly heart! doesn't allow it, or we'd put a charge of slugs in the spring-guns, and perhaps some of these beggars would get what they didn't bargain for some night.   That was Nobbs's notion, to pepper 'em up a bit; but I'm afraid we mustn't.

It wouldn't do nowadays, when every ploughboy has got a vote, and spells out a beastly Radical paper every Saturday.'

'Wouldn't it be a little feudal,' asked Harry, 'to shoot a man because he stole a wild bird for his supper?'

'I dare say it would, and a jolly good thing if we had a few more feudal institutions about to keep people in their proper places. Well, as I was telling you, we arranged a couple of these contrivances, and next day, when we took a look round, both the charges had been drawn, and a big hare was laid across the path carefully under each wire, on a little bed of bracken leaves. I suppose he'd been content to take the pheasants home. Well, that wasn't all. Nobbs was as angry as I was, I think, because the poacher had dared to make fun of him and his little dodges, and I gave Nobbs one of the hares to take home and cook. If you please, when the hare was hanging before the fire, it blew up! This led to examination of the second, which we were going to use in the kitchen, and it was found that the charge drawn from the spring-gun had been neatly packed inside the hare.'

'Quite a humorist, that poacher! But how do you know who it is?'

'No one else here has the sense to do it so cleverly. Beside, he's been seen about at all sorts of odd times, sort of reconnoitring the country. And if you go past the cottage, where his mother and daughter live, about dinner-time, and use your nose, you'll find they've always got something pretty savoury in the pot. Oh, they know what they're about, those Romanys! I remember 'em when I was a boy, when they were far more numerous out here and right into the West-Country than they are now, along all the roads from Lyme and Crewkerne and Colyton and hereabouts till you get to Cornwall. But they're all dying out or emigrating now. All your new-fangled scientific sanitary laws and your local authorities are killing 'em off between 'em.'

It has been remarked that Sir William Long was a trifle inconsistent. Though a sturdy supporter of the State Church, he persistently quarrelled with the parson. Though he hated Free Trade like the devil, he countenanced smuggling. Though he complained of not being allowed to fire slugs into gipsies, he blamed new-fangled laws for interfering with their ease and comfort.

I suppose the fact was that he objected to all laws which did not allow him to have his own way. If a man begged of him on the road, he would

damn him up hill and down dale for being a lazy,
lying, thriftless vagabond, so that the man nearly
shook out of his skin, and was sorry he spoke.
When the tall, grim, thin, powerful old squire had
got through his discourse, shaking a thick stick
at the unhappy tramp, he would suddenly say:
'There, there's half a crown for you. Much more
than you deserve. Now be off. And don't make a
beast of yourself with it, or you'll be brought before
me, and I'll see you provided with bread and water
and stone-breaking for a month.' And the tramp
would go straightway and make a whole zoological
garden of himself, but in the next county. Sir
William was very like his son in this respect, that,
if everything were put in his hands, he thought it
would be a great deal better managed than it is at
present, only he confined himself to the government of the British realm, in his criticisms, and

mentioned how he would 'give 'em what for' if he were in authority over trades-unionists, pickets, demonstrators in parks, Social Democrats, Home Rulers, teetotalers, and Radicals generally. He usually wore shabby old clothes, had his pockets full of string, rope-yarn, and shreds of cloth for nailing fruit-trees, with a few loose gun-caps and a good-sized clasp-knife, and carried a thick stick. He drank good claret and port at dinner, like a gentleman — drank plenty of them, and was never the worse. At breakfast he drank, as often as not, a cup of cider. At lunch he merely took some bread and cheese, often taking it out with him associated with the rope-yarn and gun-caps, and eating it with the clasp-knife.

In the administration of justice he was particularly happy. Once a foolish woman of the village of Redmore summoned the schoolmaster for caning

her son. Sir William, having elicited that the boy
had first stolen another boy's book and then lied
about it, said that the master was quite right, and,
'What do you pay him for, if not to teach the boy
what you don't seem to be able to teach him yourself? If the boy's to grow up a thief and a liar,
what's the use of his learning to write and to
cipher? He'll only cipher some pounds, shillings,
and pence on a bit of paper, and write somebody
else's name under it some day, and then it'll be
worse than caning. The case is dismissed, and the
schoolmaster did his duty. And, mind you!' (this
is the gem of the judgment) 'if your husband goes
and votes wrong on account of this, I'll be hanged
if I don't raise his rent.'

Such was the sturdy old baronet, of a race now
passing away—a race which cannot understand
how noblemen can be partners in tea-firms; how

anybody who does not hunt or shoot, or know how many sacks of barley ought to go to an acre, can possibly find an interest in life; why they should give up their own land to be allotted to improvident and incapable Calvinistic boors, and, above all, cannot understand how the country is going to get on without them.

He was a good friend and a formidable foe; he had some quaint opinions, and he expressed them before anybody. There was no kind of affectation or respect of persons about him, and, like old Noll's troopers, he had 'so learned to fear the Lord that he knew no other fear.'

Later in the evening Harry sat in his own room, having unpacked, to smoke a pipe and read a little before going to bed. Lowcliff was a house where people went to bed early and got up early. At ten o'clock the servants filed into the dining-room, and a lamp and book were placed on the table, and Sir William read a portion of the Scripture and a collect or two from the Liturgy, and the blessing, in a stentorian and denunciatory tone. After that a tray was put on the table with brandy, whisky, rum, glasses, water and biscuits. Sir William took rum, because the general practitioner had advised him not to, and because he thought the doctor was a fool. Then he went round the premises with a large horn lantern and saw that all the locks and bolts were shut, and the alarm-bells on curved springs of thin iron placed in their sockets on the doors and shutters. Then everyone said good-night, and Sir William went to bed with a loaded double-barrelled muzzle-loading gun standing in a corner of his dressing-room, and a long old cavalry sabre slung over the bedroom mantelpiece, with an illuminated text underneath it. And there he was at peace till a big bell over the stable began to jangle at six a.m.

Harry had a large bedroom looking out over an undulating wooded country, with an occasional cottage peeping, with a thatched roof and a little stream of blue smoke, from amid the green and purple bloom of the receding woodland, and this bedroom he also used as a private library and sitting-room, having a table in the window with writing materials, a comfortable armchair, and a book-case. He also kept a lamp of his own there, in case, as at present, he did not feel immediately disposed for sleep. The room was decorated with a few tolerable water-colours, some photographs of his family, some flowers his sister had put there the day of his arrival, and a text his mother had hung in an Oxford frame over the mantelpiece. He had added one or two photos of

public characters he admired, but there were no
girls. If he had any photos of girls at all they
were probably at his rooms at Trinity.

And he sat in his shirtsleeves (for it was hot
weather) reading a nice modern French book,
because he liked the French prose style, the happy
phrasification, and the freedom from the trammels
of conventional ethics and the melodramatic
optimism which made the English novel of the
period less completely satisfactory than it might
be. And it was all so fresh and new to him, too!

He was in that delightful condition of the clever
youth on whom the beauties of things are breaking for the first time, and constitute what is usually
called a revelation, and he was still under that
absurd but most natural impression that few people
in the world could know it all, because he had just
discovered it. There in his bookcase were De

Musset, Gautier, Baudelaire, De Banville—think of the young man of taste to whom the 'Nuit de Mai' and the 'Nuit d'Octobre,' 'Mademoiselle de Maupin' and 'Les Fleurs du Mal,' are revealed for the first time! There also (on a lower shelf, to be sure) were the joys and sorrows of Rodolphe, Schaunard, Colline and Co. There was also Villon (whom he did not know French enough to understand much of), Daudet, Bourget, and 'Atalanta in Calydon,' the 'Songs before Sunrise,' 'Dolores' and the 'Garden of Proserpine'—well, there was much more. They know who have once, a long golden age ago, been clever, imaginative, self-conscious boys themselves. And there was Heine, but Harry would have to be badly in love before he could thoroughly appreciate *him*. Wherefore we had better proceed at once to show how he got into that condition.

It was at Lady Long's garden-party the following day. ('At Home four to seven. Tennis. R.S.V.P.') He was standing on the lawn with his sister watching the people arrive, reposing for a moment from the social duties of handshaking, and saying, 'How very hot!' to the worthy neighbours who were driving up in dozens, attracted (like the wasps and bluebottles) by the renown of Sir William's fruit. The lawn was freely dotted over with different-coloured sunshades, with standing and slowly moving small groups, stout old ladies in black, tall thin old ladies in black, young ladies in white and in pink and in electric blue, clergy in long coats and tall hats, clergy in short coats and straw hats, and affable young men in indiarubber shoes carrying rackets. And every minute the numbers increased. Suddenly Harry said to his sister (who, by the

way, was very prettily attired in colours which
harmonized with the amethystine pale blue of her
eyes) :

'I say, who's that girl?'

Let us describe that girl as Harry saw her. She
was not tall, perhaps an inch shorter than his
sister. She was slender, stately, and graceful in
her movements, and wore her dress as if it grew
on her, and she had never worn another, though
this were new to-day. She had black hair, brown-
yellow eyes, large, eloquent, and innocent, and the
tropical pallor, with a tawny flame in it, which often
accompanies such hair and eyes, and a mouth of
the 'wistful' order—a mouth whose smile has an
undercurrent of sorrow, whose kiss has the power
of haunting the memory of the receiver, so that
he becomes presently mad. There is a picture in
the National Gallery where you can see that

mouth, as Harry knew. I need not say that he quoted to himself:

' Pâle comme un beau soir d'automne.'

She was dressed in sulphur colour, and wore a large black hat with feathers.

'That girl,' replied Miss Long, 'is Mrs. Vane. Come and talk to her.'

It was indeed Mrs. Vane, and, what is more, Mrs. Vane was our old friend Mary Carmen Juanita Josefina, a few years older, but girlish and feline as ever, preserving her youth though she was twenty-five, thanks, perhaps, to the fact that she was half English, and had never gone back to South America since the rather trying days of the Guano War. Her father was dead, and she had got all his money, except a portion which was her mother's for life, and as John Shindler had been a rich man, and recovered his effects from the plunder of San José, and as Pat Vane, late of the Eldorado navy, had had a good share of that plunder himself, Mrs. Vane lived very comfortably, and enjoyed herself lazily, like a cat in a nice soft silk-lined basket, her only fears being that she might some day get fat, and that her mother might come and want to stay with her.

She had been rather fond of that kindly, vulgar old father of hers; but still it was a good thing that he was permanently out of the way, as he would not have been a credit to her, and, of course, she would have Masses said for him, and could tell strangers any picturesque or pathetic fiction about his personality which might occur to her. Her mother, on the other hand, she hated, almost as much as her mother hated her. She had lived now long enough in Europe to find out that her mother was even more of a ridiculous savage than had been apparent in San José, and had had to suffer shame on her account more than once. The señora lived now in Paris, where both she and Patrick fervently trusted she would stay. Mary Carmen had now quite lost her Cockney phraseology, and had become a little Irish instead, though never losing, of course, the foreign accent, which she found a powerful auxiliary to her personal charms in England.

Harry Long was introduced to her, and she was pleased to approve of his appearance and manners, and thought that he would make a man some day —a real man—perhaps in ten years' time. In the meantime she could teach him a little of the science of life. It would amuse her—she was a little hard up for amusement—and it would do him good. Harry walked her about under the trees and among flower-beds, and sat with her on rustic benches, and gave her ices and champagne-cup, and unfolded the treasures of his intellect for her entertainment, and she knew all about him very soon.

He was in that state of adolescence in which a youth is full of the fine things he might say, if he were not too diffident to say them, or if they did not wholly go out of his head at the critical moment; while any good-looking woman who tried could get the complete mastery of his affections for the time being by the mere compliment of taking, or pretending to take, an interest in him.

And this lady did take some interest in him, and pretended more. She was not especially well educated, but she was clever, knew life better than he did in many respects, and could appreciate, or seem to understand, an unfamiliar subject without much effort. In fact, she was like a stream which is quick and sparkling, but of doubtful and variable depth. And she was the prettiest woman present, and her dress was made at least a hundred miles from Starmouth, and a hundred years in advance of Starmouth taste, and the sun shone warm, and the boy was good-looking, and evidently admired her, so she was pleased. He, of course, totally misconceived her character.

She said to Harry that he must come and see her, and explained that her husband was not present on this particular day, because he had a friend staying with him. But she added:

'You will come and see us, and if my husband is out, or busy with his friend, as he sometimes is, you will come and see me, will you not? I have so few really intellectual people to talk to, though everyone is most kind, and the country is lovely.'

This was laying it on with a trowel perhaps ; but Harry liked it. He said :

'I can quite understand. I, too, find it a privilege to converse with anyone who can talk about anything outside local gossip, and church, and politics.'

'You are not fond of politics ? No ?'

'Not the kind they grow hereabouts. I go in rather for ideas which would be considered inflammatory and subversive here. Ah, but I forgot ; you played the guitar to a Primrose meeting, I am told, so I'd better hold my peace.'

' Bah ! What do I know or care what a Primrose meeting is ? It is something about Beaconsfield, yes ? And he died when I was a little girl ' (Oh, Mary !) ' in South America. I do not know whether he was an archbishop or a general. If you like, I will play the guitar to a meeting to

encourage your political principles, whatever they
are, just as readily. I only wished to be amiable.'

'What a shame to rush you into a thing like
that ! But I hope you will some day play to a
meeting of my supporters. There will be only one
present at it, though.'

'Of course I will. Come and see me to-
morrow.'

'Thanks, awfully. What time ?'

'In the afternoon, and I will give you some tea,
or *maté*, if you prefer. Now go and attend to some
other of your guests. If you wait any longer with
me it will be remarked.'

'If you don't wish me to go, I don't care whether
it's remarked or not. I don't set a high value on
public opinion.'

'Don't you? I suppose not. When you are as
old as I am you will. *Au revoir.*' And she looked

at him with the shy sly amber eyes, and nodded, and he went away, with a hot flush, and a feeling that he had been exceptionally stupid, to offer grapes and cup to other people, to whom he was brilliant and sarcastic and superior.

And that is how it all began.

By aid of strong doses of poetry, sunsets, pale auroral afterglows, lilies, roses, stars, the countless smile of the ocean, dreams and wakeful nights, Harry managed to work himself into a perfectly wild state, and grew almost visibly thinner. He became more superior and satirical at home than ever, and occasionally indulged in hollow mirth. He looked on the hours that passed between one meeting with Mrs. Vane and another as wasted fragments of his life. He was highly pleased with himself, in reality, because the whole intrigue was constructed exactly on the model of some of his favourite works. Mrs. Vane was a married woman, that was the first distinct point in its favour, and he chose to consider her 'mated to a clown'; albeit perhaps, if he had known a little more about poor Pat Vane, he might have withdrawn that aspersion, though it is true Patrick had grown a good deal fatter and redder, and had got a little too fond of John Jamieson. Then there was the delightful personality of his idol, and he thought he knew what *câlinerie* meant now. To do the lady justice, she was only playing, while Harry was in high-toned anapæstic frenzy. She did not permit him any except the most trivial and tantalizing freedom of behaviour. She liked him, but was not at all disturbed in her sleep or appetite on his account.

The fortunate part, too, was that Harry's parents never found out the foolishness which he was proudly carrying on. It never entered into their heads to conceive such a thing. She was a married lady, and he was a young gentleman of England, and their son, wherefore it was unimaginable that there should be 'anything between them.' Respectable young gentlemen did not make love to married ladies in a country which enjoys the blessings of a Protestant Succession, an Established Church, and a virtuous Royal Family. Sir William and Lady Long had been well 'brought up' after the fashion of their time, so that no great violence of sexual passion had ever come within their ken. She had been the daughter of a 'gentleman of property' in Hampshire, and he had 'formed an attachment' to her (she having been thrown into his society to that end), after which he had 'expressed his admiration,' to her parents, of her 'person and manners,' which were 'agreeable,' if a trifle silly, and obtained their permission (which they were overjoyed to grant) to 'make his proposals' or 'pay his addresses' to the lady. I am not certain that he did not make or pay them in writing, with his crest at the top, and 'your most obt. and devotd. admirer' at the bottom, and beginning 'Madam,' so that it was all done most properly and genteelly, and never went much above the recognised degree of tepidity.

Consequently, they were far from likely to suppose their son capable of 'carrying on an intrigue' founded on romances they had never read or heard of, and pursued in a spirit unknown to them. Bessie had some inkling of the matter, and smiled to herself, and waited what the end would be.

So for a little while Harry had a delightful excursion into that frequently-explored, but

always new and attractive region called Fools'
Paradise.

And then Shaw came, who will be further
treated of.

But before Shaw came Harry's horn was exalted,
and he patted himself on the back and told himself
he was no end of a dog, and that he really had
better look out; he was going rather far, but it was
fate after all, and 'come what may, there was one
thing worth,' etc. (only it is doubtful whether he
ever got it). It is usual on these occasions to
blame fate.

One evening, after dinner, Harry set forth with
a cigarette, in the time of sunset, for a stroll in
the grounds. He liked to wander out by himself
to think. He thought about Mrs. Vane, and about
himself, and planned what he would say to her,
and what he would do when they met again, as

he hoped would be the case to-morrow.   There
was a landing-place, I mentioned, on the river, at
the bottom of the sloping wood belonging to
Crowhill, and just in shore, hidden among the
oak-trees, an old summer-house.   Here Mrs. Vane
had provided some comfortable basket-chairs, and
here she was in the habit, on fine warm afternoons,
of sitting, reading novels, eating sweets, and rolling
cigarillos with little orange-dyed finger and thumb
tips.   And if Harry Long paddled down in a canoe
so far, she would nod to him lazily and smile, and
perhaps throw a chocolate cream at him, as if he
were a waterfowl come to be fed.   Then he would
come ashore, and she would point to a chair, and
say : ' Sit down, and make yourself comfortable.
Now amuse me.'   Then Harry would become
dumb with self-torture to extract that flow of
airy epigram which came to him so easily

when he was by himself imagining conversations.

Very well, he was alone in the evening, taking a stroll in the grounds of Lowcliff. In the course of time he got into a shady copse with grassy paths, called Joan's Grove, from some story connected with it, where a fair amount of game was usually to be found, and where some coops were, in pheasant-breeding time, under the jealous care of Pentony Nobbs, the keeper. The path was covered with rich, thick mossy grass, which made his footsteps silent, and he walked slowly on, inhaling the fragrance of the summer evening. The path he followed would lead him to a gate—an ordinary five-barred gate, fastened with a hurdle ring; and beyond the gate was a barley-field, sloping down towards the Lowcliff side of the river.

Crowhill was a mile or so lower down, and on

the opposite side. The river at Lowcliff was narrow and shallow, and only navigable in summer by a canoe.

Before the path reached the gate it bent a good deal to the left, and as Harry was in the act of rounding the bend, he met and nearly came in collision with a girl—the girl Lee whom he had seen in the cottage garden, with her grandmother, the day he came home. So she was trespassing; and, what was worse, she was carrying an animal, to wit, a rabbit, in one hand, and a very obvious wire in the other. She stood still, and stared defiantly out of dark eyes at Harry, and he looked curiously at her. If she ran away, the gate would stop her long enough for him to catch her. If she tried to dodge past him, he would probably trip her up. Besides, even if she escaped success-fully, she could easily be identified and found at home. Distinctly a tight place—what the burglar calls 'a fair cop.' So she stared defiantly at Harry, and breathed a little quickly. Besides, she liked looking at Harry, and felt, if she were to be 'run in' at all, she would rather he did it than the keeper or the constable. She had the vaguest ideas of the penalty attached to her crime. It might be six months, and it might be two years; there might or might not be arduous mechanical exertion attached to it. And only for having a lark, after all, she reflected, and taking a rabbit worth fourpence no one would ever miss.

'Well, Miss Lee, this is rather cool, isn't it?'

Miss Lee offered no remark.

'May I ask *why* you take other people's rabbits?'

'Because we've got none of our own, and want some.'

Eva Lee did not know that she had put Socialism in a nutshell. Harry said:

'Well, it's lucky for you, under the circumstances, that I'm not my father.'

'It's lucky for you, sir, I wasn't mine. I say, are you going to take me to the keepers, and the police, and Starmouth lock-up, and all that? I'll go with you quietly, if you want.'

And there was a sad animal submission in the dark eyes, visible, though the twilight grew. Harry smiled, and replied:

'Look here, you can take the bunny home with you, and I'll keep it dark! Don't let old Nobbs spot you, though, or there'll be the deuce to pay.'

The dark eyes lighted up with a splendid smile, and the girl said in a low voice:

'God bless you, sir! And I'll never take a bird or beast of yours again—strike me blind!'

'I say,' added Harry hesitatingly, 'if it isn't a rude question, you're a gipsy by birth, aren't you?'

'Yes, sir.'

'Well, do you know anything about fortune-telling—hand-reading, you know?'

'Oh yes, grandmother taught me something of *dukkerin*, but it's all nonsense! She used to get a little money out of *gorgios* at race-meetings by it. It's mostly nonsense. I've been to school, and I know better.'

'Well, I don't doubt there's a good deal of non-sense in it—sometimes; but I should take it as a favour if you would read mine, to the best of your ability.'

'Not for money?'

'No. For—for a lark.'

Eva Lee hesitated, then suddenly seemed to make up her mind.

'Give me your left hand.'

And he stood, as a patient having his pulse felt stands, while she bent closely over his hand in the fading light. A very pretty picture.

'You must come nearer the gate. I can't see under these trees.'

And they went. Eva Lee again took his hand, leaning her own elbow on the gate, and inspected Harry's 'lines.'

'Awfully pretty girl!' reflected he, as he waited for the verdict. 'If I was a bounder I should take advantage of the position to try and kiss her.'

The girl stood up, relinquished his hand, and said:

'You want what you can't get. If you do get it, you will be sorry, till something else makes you glad you lost it.'

'That's rather oracular, isn't it?'

'How do you mean?'

'Couldn't you put it a little plainer?'

'You love a woman who doesn't love you, and you don't love a woman yet who—does.'

Harry started.

'Go on.'

'And there are two deaths—but not yours. You will suffer, and then you will be happy, and wiser and stronger for sorrow.'

'Of course you can't tell me who any of these people are?'

'No. I can't tell that. There's old Nobbs's voice, in the wood, talking to his dog!'

'I don't hear anything.'

'No, sir, you're not a gipsy—and a poacher. Good-night! Thank you, always and always. *Kushto bak!*'

And Miss Lee was over the gate and going along the dry ditch of the barley-field, hidden by the hedge, in no time. Shortly Pentony Nobbs appeared with a dog and gun, and gave Harry good-evening.

CHAPTER III.

THE next day Harry went in the afternoon in his canoe down the river, under the delightful shade of trees, with the sunlight falling through in spots and moving spirals and aureoles on the water, alongside green meadows sloping gently down, where the river began to widen, and the green rushes to stand in stiff little groups at the soft crumbling edges, under bowing trees again, and so on to the old wooden landing-place of Crowhill, where he paused and looked in the accustomed direction. But the old arbour was empty. The chairs were still there, but the charmer was gone. This was the first shock.

Puzzled, he got out of his canoe, and, tying it to the little pier, walked up the winding path through the wood which led to the house, thinking of the last time he had walked along it with her, and of the things which had been said at the different parts of it, of which the various trees, turnings, and even exposed roots and casual stones, were lasting landmarks. And as he walked a germ of dread was born in his mind: would this whispering wood of memories, these fragrant fragments of fair summer scenes, be one day all that was left to him of this first love of his? Would the lonely old red house among the fir-trees be an uninscribed monument to the departed joy, the tender sorrow, and the eternal memory of a star-crossed passion, a place he would come again from far countries to see, when stern maturity had replaced his romantic youth, to yearn again for the far-off days, the fairy tale, all lilies and roses and running sunlit water, which he had once lived? And then he thought again, in this solitary copse, of still earlier days, when the old white-headed parson, now dead, used to preach in a black gown, and he, a little boy, sang every Sunday afternoon, in the growing winter twilight, to the old tune—

'Swift to its close ebbs out life's little day;
Earth's joys grow dim, its glories pass away;'

and then he and Bessie used to come home and have jam for tea. Somehow his throat got tearful. And all this because Mrs. Vane, whom he had no business to love at all, was not in the arbour. He went to the house, and rang at the bell. It was answered by the tall, dark, soldierly servant, Lee, whose functions seemed various. Harry asked, with the diffidence of youth, if Mr. Vane were at home, and was told that they were all gone out in the yacht. Then his spirits revived, and he thought: 'Well, there's nothing particular in that, though they might have given me the refusal too. But perhaps Vane's jealous.' Buoyed up with that soothing idea, he asked Lee how long they would be away, and he replied that he was not certain, but not more than a day or two, he understood. So Harry withdrew, and returned to his canoe in somewhat higher spirits, thinking what a very unnecessary owl he had made of himself a few minutes before.

And he let himself drift slowly down the creek, reflecting with complacent melancholy that

> ' Even the weariest river
> Winds somewhere safe to sea.'

When he got down to Starmouth, the bay, the

little gray stone dock and breakwater, the black-hulled fishing smacks and ketches with sails half hoisted and loose to dry—sails the colour of autumn leaves, the nets coloured like tobacco of different strengths, from black Cavendish to tawny Turkish, with bleached cork discs attached—the old stone lodging cottages, the narrow esplanade supported by a rough gray wall, the white and yellow shingle, and the far-spread mysterious motionless blue water, lay all in the shadeless radiance of the southern afternoon, and ever so far away in the vapour that veiled the horizon was something small and white, like the white of the wings of a sea-gull. And that was the main-sail and gaff-topsail and spinnaker of the *Ierne*, gliding slowly into invisibility. It was so calm that she had been hours getting those few miles away.

For the next day or two Harry haunted Starmouth Bay, and I dare say the constant exposure to air and water and the exercise did him a great deal of good. He scanned the 'offing' with the vigilance of a coastguard, bringing a small single-barrelled telescope to bear on the different craft. During the second afternoon of being thus em-ployed, he suddenly and remorsefully recollected that Shaw was to come, and that he ought to be at the station to meet him. However, it was too late now, and he could only hope that they had been more thoughtful up at the house, as in fact they had. His sister had mentioned it after lunch, when she saw Harry go towards the river in flannel array, and evidently with his mind full of some-thing other than Shaw, and Rogers had been sent with the dogcart.

Harry's persistency was rewarded by the sight of the *Ierne* at last, coming in almost before the wind,

for though still a warm fine day, a 'depression'
was advancing from Spain, and the south-east
calm was changing into a south-south-western
breeze, and a ripple was spreading over the
Channel. Erelong she took up her moorings in
good style, the sails came down, and after a little
while a boat came alongside, a smart brown
varnished boat; and down the little ladder, where
the white hand-ropes and oval fenders hung, came
—a lady (Mrs. Vane), a gentleman, another gentleman, and then Mr. Vane, and they were pulled
towards the shore.

This was the second shock.

Of course they would go up to the landing in
the creek, which was out of sight round the bend,
so Harry posted himself and canoe as if on his
way home, in such wise that the boat must pass
him. He wanted to see her face again, and he

wanted to see the two strangers, and he wanted to know what it all meant. In due course they came, the sunburnt handsome young mariners in blue guernseys, with *Ierne* in white letters on the breast, and blue stocking-caps, pulling in short, powerful salt-water arm-strokes, so different from the river-pulling Harry was accustomed to see about Grassy and Ditton. Suddenly Harry had a brilliant thought. Those men, of course, would go to one of the Starmouth taverns, as soon as they had done their work, to the Pilot-boat, the Ship, the King's Arms, the London, the New Inn, the Let the Bees Live, or the Ring o' Bells. What would be easier than at the expense of a little refresh-ment to pump one of them as to the voyage and the passengers? It was a nice quiet, tricky, detective sort of thing to do. Was it quite gentle-manly? Oh, that be somethinged! all was fair in—— There! now he was dropping into proverbs, which showed that something was getting seriously wrong with his brains.

Mrs. Vane in the boat saw him, and nodded, and smiled sweetly. She had on a white cap, of the kind called *beret* in France, and known in England as a Carlist cap, and later as a Leonardo da Vinci cap, and it became her. Vane, in a blue serge suit, held the yoke-lines, and nodded good - humouredly, and called out, ' Lovely weather !'

The two strange gentlemen were of this appearance. One was stalwart and broad-shouldered, and had a bullet head, short hair like a soldier, and a square, leathery-skinned face, with a shortish nose, and masterful chin under a thick moustache of a grizzled brown, slightly resembling, in total effect, the popular caricature of Bismarck. The reader will perhaps recognise Señor Don Miguel Doherty, a few years older, though, of course, Harry had no idea who he could be. That youth would have been pleased to hear Captain Doherty say to Vane: 'Who's that, now?' and Vane reply: 'Oh, he's a clever boy—a neighbour of ours here. Mary knows more of him than I do, for he's a great mash of hers.'

The other stranger was a small man, with regular, somewhat Oriental features, a sallow complexion, very black hair, straight like an Indian's, a small moustache produced laterally in thin spikes, a rather foreign cut of clothes, and a general air of dainty neatness. He had remarkably expressive brown eyes set in black-lashed, deep orbits—eyes that looked as if they were not accustomed to miss anything there might be to see. His age would be difficult to guess, but he looked younger than Doherty or Vane, and Harry put him down as quite a young man.

Meanwhile, Miss Elizabeth Long had decided that the afternoon would be best spent in a hammock she had had slung between two shady trees in the garden, with the cat and 'Treasure Island;' and there is no doubt she was more sensibly occupied than her brother. And just as she had got to the part where the ship is being fitted out, and a crew found at the port of Bristol, someone came silently over the lawn towards her, making a moving obstruction to the sunlight which her eyes absently saw without noticing. Not wishing to startle her, the someone coughed, and the cat got up, and fidgeted and trampled round and round, and Bessie looked up with a surprised smile, and saw a man in a pale-brown tweed suit, who took off his hat, and said :

'Don't get up, Miss Long. I hope I didn't startle you. The servant sent me out here, thinking that Long—that your brother was somewhere about here. I hope you know who I am?'

'Of course I know who you are;' and she sat up in the hammock, ejected the cat, which stretched itself regretfully and blinked, jumped out herself, and shook hands with the visitor, looking welcome and some quiet merriment from those eyes, which he compared mentally to pale cornflowers.

'Father and mother are out, and Harry's canoeing, but he'll be in directly. Would you like to have anything?'

'Oh, I think not, thanks.'

'I think you would. You have come a long way, and it's a hot day. If you were in your rooms in Trinity College, you would send the gyp out for a tankard of college ale, on a day like this, I'm sure.'

'Well, it is rather hot, certainly, but——'

'Come along.' And Miss Long led the way in at the open French window of the breakfast-room, and said: 'Now, you sit down there, and wait a minute, if you'll excuse me.'

And Shaw sat down and waited, and smiled gently, and murmured in the depths of his soul: 'Very few other girls would have had so much sense.' J. R. Shaw was a man of a trifle over thirty, about five feet ten, sallow complexion, thick brown hair, parted in the middle, and tending to curl a little at the sides and back when it had not just been cropped short, a longish straight nose, thin face, and a brown moustache of a lighter colour than his hair. He wore glasses, attached to a very thin gold cord, and his gray eyes had, in addition to the rather tired look peculiar to short-sighted people who read a good deal, a keenly humorous expression, as if the whole world were something very funny indeed, if you could only see it through his glasses. People used to say: 'He's not handsome, and yet it's a face you can't help liking.'

He was square-shouldered, but had the slight stoop of reading men who are rather tall. He had long slender brown hands, and wore no rings or gloves. Some years ago he had been a scholar, and then he had taken a place in the first class of the Classical Tripos, upon which he became a coach. Recently he had taken his M.A., and the white name on a black ground on the wall at the bottom of his staircase had been duly altered from ' J. R. Shaw ' to ' Mr. Shaw.' He looked forward, with some sadness, to a fellowship at ' some small college pervaded with piety and black men,' by-and-by.

And Bessie came in again with a small salver, on which was a tankard of ale.

' There,' she said.

'.Thanks, so much! What a very fine tankard !'

' It's more than a century old. Very few people ever are allowed to use it.'

' Thanks again.' And he drank.

When he put it down, with a grateful sigh, she said :

' Now, would you like to come and walk about the garden ?'

' Yes. There is only one thing I should like better than walking in the garden.'

' What's that ?'

' Well—sitting in the garden.'

'You are lazy.'

'Yes, very.'

'Can you walk as far as the seat under the elm, do you think?'

'Man might try.'

'I hope you're not going to encourage Harry to be lazy.'

'Oh no! He shall work. Oh, by all means! He shall practise sprinting, and I'll keep the time.'

'But I mean for his Tripos.'

'Oh! I thought you meant tennis and that sort of thing—the things men do in flannels in hot weather. His Tripos is all right. At least, it ought to be, if he doesn't spread out too much after fads. He's far too original.'

'Too original?'

'Yes. It's getting such a common trick now among undergraduates to be original.'

' Weren't you ?'

' No.   I was abjectly commonplace.   I tubbed,
I had a green tablecloth from Swann's, I rowed in
the fourth First Trinity five, was bumped by Lady
Margaret, and photo'd in a group by Hills and
Saunders with our names underneath.   I quoted
Macaulay's essays at the Union—quoted them so
copiously that they made me President—and always
voted Tory.'

' I hope you do still.'

' Yes ; I'm so commonplace that I do still.   I
shot at a target, too, and attacked hedges in
skirmishing order.   Oh, I was a very ordinary
man !'

' But you got a first class?   That's not
ordinary.'

' No.   Though attempts at it sometimes lead to
the Ordinary by Special permission.   But lots of

men get first-classes every year. Don't press my proposition too hard, or it will give way.' And Shaw leaned back on the rustic seat under the big old elm, and extended his legs some distance to his front on the soft green lawn, and looked pleased.

'This is very nice, after four hours' joggling in the South-Western, and one and a half in the Great Eastern. You ought to be very happy, living in a place like this. I suppose you are?'

'Oh yes, I think so. At least, I never think about it.'

'That is a good sign. It's a mistake to begin analyzing and wondering whether you're really happy. You get to doubting whether it's worth while being alive at all, then you begin thinking about the meaning of things in general, and so work your mind into a state wherein you demand passionately why effect should be the consequence of cause.'

' They say it's selfish, too, to let your mind be taken up by things like that, that you ought to find your happiness by not seeking it, in making other people happy. I don't say I'm like that, you know, only that they say one ought to be.'

' Yes. I've heard of that method of ethics too. Perhaps it is a little weak in places. Yes. When you come to think of it, it is inconsistent with itself. That's where it breaks down.'

' How ?'

' Well, you can't be unselfish, and make a sacrifice for another, unless another is selfish enough to accept it. Without selfishness on one side, unselfishness on the other doesn't come off, any more than steel without flint.'

' It doesn't sound right, somehow. I don't think many people would agree to that.'

' Then it's all the more likely to be true. Don't you see? Suppose you had one chocolate cream— have you one? It would make the illustration more convincing.'

' No. Wish I had. I shouldn't give it to you.'

' No ; I give you credit for that. But suppose you were one of those altruistic people, and wanted me to take it, though you would like it yourself, wouldn't I be a beast to accept it ?'

' Of course, because I should only offer it out of politeness, and expect you to refuse it.'

' But that is an evasion of my hypothesis. And if I don't take it, what becomes of your altruism ? The motive remains, of course, to increase the sum of your good intentions ; but what's the good of a system of ethics which can't translate intention into action without encouraging in one person the quality it prohibits in another?'

'Well, what would you do if things were the other way?'

'I? Oh, I should eat it, I suppose!'

'I know what you would really do—you would say you had a lot more, and didn't really want it, and that would enable me to accept it without selfishness.'

'I think a neat essay might be written on the egotism of unselfish people, who must always indulge their vice at the expense of the moral integrity of others.'

Bessie smiled a little, and looked at the flower-beds a little way off in the sunlit part of the lawn. Then she looked at Shaw with a comical expression, and asked:

'Do you still worship idols?'

'Gracious! do you remember that? Oh, I'm more advanced now. I've got a cat.'

'Are you fond of cats?'

'Yes; I like cats very much.'

'So do I. What becomes of her in your absence?'

'The bedmaker looks after her. She's very affectionate—I mean the bedmaker is—and Jezebel is gone to board with her for the Long.'

'*What* do you call her?'

'Jezebel; also Pasht. But the bedmaker calls her Kitty.'

Here Harry came over the lawn, having learnt in the house of Shaw's arrival, saying:

'Hullo, Shaw! Glad to see you! I say, I'm awfully sorry I wasn't in when you came, but it's rather a grind getting up here from the bay against the stream. Have you been looked after all right?'

'Very much so, thanks.'

'Why, you're not even smoking! What on earth are you thinking about, Bessie?'

'I'm very sorry. It didn't occur to me.'

'And it didn't occur to me either, Miss Long. It's all right.'

'Well, would you like to sit here, Shaw, or to go and loaf about a bit?'

'Just as you like.'

'Well, let's go for a turn and have a pipe. We dine at seven, and it's a quarter-past five now, so there's plenty of time.'

'All right.'

Bessie discreetly disappeared.

'Did you manage the travelling all right, Shaw?'

'Fairly well. From Waterloo to Bishopstoke

was of a bustling, express order. At Bishopstoke—no, I think it was Basingstoke; make it so—one examined the scenery a good deal. Some pretty leisurely skirmishing across country towards Salisbury, very rural. I had no idea England could be so rural—I mean so entirely destitute of square brick houses with blue slate roofs. At Salisbury one ate something, and drank ale. What a very charming place you have here, Long!'

'Yes, it's a jolly old place, isn't it? And it's something to have the river and sea handy. If this weather lasts, we'll bathe daily. Come and do it now, if you like.'

' Will there be time ?'

'Oh yes. It isn't far to the seashore, only it's uphill going home. I generally canoe, but, unfortunately, that won't do for two, and it doesn't take so long to walk.'

'Very well. Only you are responsible for my being back here in time to change.'

So they went, and admired the quaint beauty of steep Starmouth town and its sunny bay, where they plunged and gambolled joyously in the transparent green and purple water, not from a bathing-machine, in which case a long walk over sand and stones and weedy water up to his ankles is the bather's portion, but from a boat, manned by one of those lazy, brown, peaceful-eyed men in dark blue guernseys, who seem to spend their time standing on the shore and spitting, when not visiting a lobster-pot in the early morning. Harry knew this man, and asked him if he knew where the *Ierne*, now moveless at her moorings, with hull a-glitter in south-western sunlight, had been to. The man replied that he was told somewhere about near the Isle of Wight, but added:

'But, law there! they Irish chaps'll tell any lie. Dan Bere's smack was out early s'marnin, and 'e says as 'e see 'er comin' from the coast o' France, and then she putt 'er 'ellum' (somewhere Harry didn't understand or remember), 'and shifted 'er course a matter o' fower pints; but, there, I s'pose they knows their own business best.'

'That's odd,' said Shaw. 'Who does she belong to? She's a very pretty cutter.'

'Ah, she be!' said the mariner; 'and she can walk too.'

'She belongs to Mr. Vane, of Crowhill, a neighbour of ours,' said Harry, as he pulled off his shirt over his head.

'Oh! There was a fellow-passenger of mine, the only one who got out at what's-its-name.'

'Shervil?'

'Shervil, yes. And he wanted to go to Crowhill. You'd think him a Scotchman—shrewd reader—at sight. We conversed in the train a little. He seemed a person of wide experience of what I call an out-door kind. Not exactly cultured, you know, in the midnight oil sense—I should think the midnight whisky more in his line—but he had once known what they call Humahnities, and added to that much knowledge of *urbes* and *gentes*. Dark, long party. Military exterior. Tendency to haggle with local fly-driver. All of which formed a mild entertainment for me. Good-day!'

And Shaw's lank person, decorated simply with a pair of gold spring double-glasses, precipitated itself head first over the stern. Harry saw him, and went better.

As they walked home, refreshed, and enjoying the warm sun, Shaw observed :

' I met a man called Vane once.'

' Did you?　Where?'

' In Paris.'

' When?'

' Last Easter Vac.'

' What was he like?'

' Shortish, dull red as to hair and moustache, with gray striations. Bulged some, as the Americans say, about the waist. Placable, given to conversation of an autobiographic kind, and to strange drinks. The latter in excess, like acids in analysis. He spoke after the manner of the western member of the group composing the British archipelago, and, like my friend in the train to-day, seemed to know all about Grand Cathay—he was distinctly a Cataian in the Shakespearian sense—and the land of Prester John.'

' But that's the man!'

' You know him, eh ? Then you know also Mary Carmen Juanita Intimidad Larrañaga, and so forth ?'

' Mrs. Vane ? Yes, I know her.'

' So do I. Perhaps you — I say, is it serious ?'

' Fairly serious,' replied Harry with bashful pride.

' Has she played the guitar to you ?'

' Yes.'

' Has she told you you were the only person who could really understand her ?'

' Well, yes. Why ?'

' Oh, it's what she used to tell me ! I wanted to find out if she had developed any new methods since. She managed to convey to me how beautiful and clever I was, till I nearly believed it, and she cost me at least a hundred francs in bangles and sweets and junketings. What has she got you to buy for her?'

' Well, you couldn't buy much here if you wanted. I have given her a few sweets, perhaps, and a little tobacco—and—er—a cigarette-holder.'

' Any gloves?'

' Oh yes, a pair or two!'

' And you've known her—how long?'

' Well, ever since I came down.'

' That is nearly a fortnight. Now, you take my tip, as the vulgar say, and turn it up.'

' That's all very well, but I don't quite see it. After all, it isn't any very great harm if she has had a few little things. She takes a child-like delight in those trifles, and probably does not know what they cost—why, she is hardly more than a child.'

At the same time Harry had received the third shock of this shockful day.

'Child? She is a South American, and has been a woman for the last fourteen years, and probably had more lovers than she can count or remember. She is just as shallow, vain, and selfish as they are made. Don't imagine I am moralizing. I merely mean she is not good enough. I regret to say, also, that she has no conception of the sanctity of truth. I could give instances.'

'You have evidently got a strong prejudice against her.'

'All right. Make it so. You will find out for yourself. I say, do you put on evening-dress for dinner?'

'No. I mean yes.'

And Harry became meditative and depressed. Shaw smiled as he sat at the table later on, and encouraged Sir William in his political and social views, and talked about the General Election. Shaw was a young philosophic Tory of the modern type. The orthodox modern Liberal has a kind of contemptuous affection for the 'regular fossilized old Tory,' of the class Sir William Long might be said to belong to; but he hates and fears the young and cultivated individualist Tory, whose weapon is polished ridicule instead of pious denunciation, for the orthodox modern Liberal knows that he must be serious, that his supporters are nearly all serious people, of Calvinistic tendencies, and Social Democrats whose strong point is rarely a sense of humour. Consequently, he thoroughly enjoys being made to wriggle on the barbed hook of polite sarcasm backed by wide culture. It is not half so bad to be thought wicked by the old school as to be thought absurd by the new.

Sir William enjoyed Shaw very much, and made

him premise to help in the forthcoming election. It should be said that a General Election was about to take place that summer, on a question which was entirely new to the country, and far more sensational than the old Local-Option-Deceased-Wife's-Sister-Allotment kind of contests, and marvellous rumours were flying about. For it was the great Home Rule election, and anything, from civil war downwards, was considered possible in the course of the next few months.

And Harry sat very impatient through all this, for his mind was otherwhere.

It was a very hot evening, and one of the longest of the year, the sun not setting till about twenty minutes past eight, and soon after dinner most of the party went out into the garden to enjoy the slightly cooler air, and to admire the sunset, far away, at the wood-fringed ridge of the farther slope of the valley—a sandy red and yellow sunset, graduating up through greenish brown and indigo to unstained blue, which clad all the distant trees on the hill-top, hiding Crowhill in a golden dust of light for a few fleeting moments, after which they became black outlines against a saffron and peach-green afterglow.

Lady Long put on a crochet shawl as a precaution against the night air. It made her very uncomfortable and was wholly unnecessary, but she had been taught from her earliest youth to take invariable precautions against some mysterious venom lurking in that night air, which, of course, she knew to be of entirely different composition and properties to the day air. Bessie had made no addition to her indoor costume, which was a cream-coloured muslin frock with a canary-silk sash.

Mr. Shaw had put on a short black velvet coat

and a small cloth travelling cap of particularly
hideous colour and shape, with which he appeared
pleased, and was by permission smoking a large
drooping briar pipe, of a glossy rich dark brown,
silver-gilt and amber-mouthed. Miss Long was
wishing she knew him well enough to ask whether
it was not the weight of it which caused him to
stoop slightly.

Sir William had changed his black coat for his
homely shooting-jacket, with the familiar pockets
full of the familiar useful articles, had put on a
straw hat, very faded, and bent in the brim, and
gone for a little walk along the side of a field or
two, and through the woods. Harry, in a First
Trinity 'blazer and straw,' had loafed with a
cigarette on the lawn for a minute or two; then,
seeing Shaw fully occupied in talking to Bessie,
and not wishing to have a long protracted con-

versation with his mother about petunias and what she called 'pelargon'ums,' quietly disappeared to enjoy a little solitude along the towing-path, as it might be called, though very little was ever towed there. It was simply a narrow public road alongside the river, and the estate of Lowcliff reached down to this road, where it was bounded by a rough stone wall of varying height. The ground on the Lowcliff side was near the level of the top of the wall, so that in order to get into the road one simply need jump three or four feet down, whereas to get into Lowcliff from the road one must climb three or four feet up. Neither process presenting any special difficulty to Harry, he jumped down, with the intention of walking alongside the river awhile in poetic melancholy and meditation, and climbing up at a point which would bring him back to the house by a different route.

But when he sprang down, he pitched, strange to say, almost on the toes of a young woman who was walking or standing in the road, who jumped and said, 'Oh!' It was gradually getting dark, but not so much so as to prevent his recognising the heroine of the rabbit and the wire whom education had led to despise *dukkerin*, though not apparently to forget that art.

'I beg your pardon!' said Harry. 'Oh, it's you, Miss Lee! I'm awfully sorry. Hope I didn't startle you?'

'No, sir,' replied Eva Lee.

'Which way are you going?'

'I was going home, sir, to Redmore.'

'Where I saw you in the garden with your hands full of flowers the day I came?'

'Yes, sir.'

'That's up the river, and then turn up to the

right at the stile beyond Joan's Grove, I pre-
sume ?'

The girl turned hot at the mention of the scene
of her recent exploit, and said :

' Yes, sir.'

' Oh, don't call me " sir "; it's ridiculous !   It
sounds as if I were a sort of feudal chieftain.   Look
here, I'm going along your way !   If you'll allow
me, I'll go with you as far as the stile, and then
I must go in.'

' Better not, Mr. Long,' said the girl.

' Why ?'

' Someone might see you, and you wouldn't
like that.'

' I don't the least care; I'm doing nothing to
be ashamed of; and unless, of course, you don't
want me, I should be delighted.'

' I don't mean I wouldn't like you to——'

'Then, if you please, what do you mean?' pursued Harry, standing and smiling, with his hat pushed back from his forehead, and his hands in his pockets, his unbuttoned flannel jacket showing his white evening shirt and single diamond stud. It certainly was a hot evening.

The girl said:

'I wonder you should want to talk to me, or risk being seen with me. I'm a gipsy, and nothing better than a tramp, except that I've been to school, and we have a house to live in now; and you know I'm a thief,' she added in a low voice, with a deeper tinge of colour which was hardly perceptible in the dusk, 'and you a gentleman, and one that will have a title some day.'

'Some distant day, I hope. But that's all rot, Miss Lee! I wouldn't worry about that if I were you. I expect it was only a lark, and, anyhow, I think the game laws are very absurd. Come along.' And the girl obeyed, and they walked on, she rather silent and probably shy, Harry making conversation about the weather and the scenery as he would have done for a girl in his own 'station in life' whose acquaintance he had recently made, and whose diffidence he wished to dispel by ignoring its causes. It is true he was a little self-conscious in this, and rather too deliberately gentlemanly and elaborately chivalrous, but that is excusable. In conversation and on paper he scorned *grands seigneurs*, but he quite enjoyed being regarded as one; and as he glanced from time to time at the girl who walked beside him—tall, upright, lissom, and graceful without effort, with the grace of a Dryad, a daughter of the Woods and the Sun, whose sisters the Wind and Water were—Harry thought that perhaps, after all, there was something shallow, something artificial, about Mrs. Vane. And he turned to his Dryad —a Dryad in a nineteenth-century garb which had seen better days—and said: 'How do you amuse yourself all day? Do you do work, or what?'

'I sometimes go on a message for father or grandmother, and to fetch things, and I look after the garden. That's the only work I do. Father wants me to go and be a servant at — where he is.'

'I know. Well?'

'Yes, I expect you do.'

'What do you mean?'

'Nothing. Only you go there, calling and so on, don't you?'

'Oh yes! I'm there now and then. But you were saying——'

'I wouldn't go and be a servant there at any price, or anywhere, if I could help it. Of course, if I had to—to earn my living, well, I should just have to, and that'd be an end. But I want to be out-of-doors.'

'Quite right, too. But you seem to have a special antipathy to Crowhill?'

'I don't think I know what antipathy means.'

'Well, dislike—the opposite of sympathy.'

'Oh, I hate the place!'

'Do you? Would you mind telling me why?'

"It's unlucky. There's what grandmother calls a bad *duk* on it.'

'Your father doesn't seem to mind that.'

'Father's been a soldier, and been all over the world, and isn't afraid of anything—not of anything at all.'

'That's rather like my father, in a way. He's

been a soldier, and he's been in several parts of the world, and he certainly isn't afraid of anything.'

'Then it'd be rather a bad job for them to meet—way you and me did, wouldn't it?' replied the Dryad, with something approaching dry humour.

'Well, perhaps it would. Let's hope it won't come off. By the way, did you mention that accidental occurrence to any of your people?'

'No, I didn't. It was no business of theirs, and I kept it to myself. They'd have only laughed at you, and I wouldn't have them do that.'

'Well, I think you were right. But is that the only reason you dislike Crowhill, because your grandmother says it's unlucky? I thought you rather sniffed at that particular species of superstition the other day?'

'I told you most *dukkerin* was nonsense, just a dodge to get money out of ladies and gentlemen and servant-girls, and so it is. I suppose you'd be surprised to hear your servants come to grandmother to have their *duks* told?'

'By Jove, that's rather good! No, I wasn't aware of it. Which ones?'

'You won't tell, because I believe it's a police business?'

'No, of course I won't tell.'

'Well, Mary and Eliza came first together. They were in no end of a fright, and grandmother burnt some salt and sulphur and spirits in a pot— it was evening, you know, and they said they'd leave out to go to chapel—and charged them a shilling each. She gave 'em lovely *duks*, but they went away with their teeth all of a rattle.'

'Excellent old lady!'

' Then one day Mr. Rawlins came.'

' *Rawlins!* Good heavens ! Well ?'

It might be mentioned that Rawlins belonged
to the race of ancient and attached servants. He
was a butler, officially. As a human reality, he
was a shambling, red-nosed, useless, glassy-eyed
wreck, who helped himself freely to Sir William's
choicest liquors; was far too dazed to pour anything
out with safety, and shook visibly when visitors
asked him if Lady Long was at home. In his less
vacuous moments he was dictatorial and pious.
He cultivated several complaints with great pride,
and when his own health, or anyone else's, was
inquired after, gave the dismallest possible accounts,
introducing as much unsavoury detail as possible.
When Sir William (in robust health and good
spirits) had started off for a walk of eight miles
or so up and down hill, Rawlins would say :

'Master, 'e seems to be lookin' up a bit. 'E don't find it quite so 'ard to get about a little. Yes; 'e's a trifle easier this afternoon, but 'e'll never be the same man agen.'

Miss Eva Lee said :

' Well, we thought it funny, too.'

' And did he want his rotten old destiny unravelled ? I hope you gave it him warm.'

' He wanted physic, to begin with. He looked as if he wanted it badly. Grandmother gave him some muck or other — she knows a lot about medicine and diseases—and I'm afraid he paid for it with a bottle of gin that came out of your cellar.'

' I should think that was extremely likely. And I have no doubt he lectures the slaveys on superstition, and honesty, and temperance, and that sort of thing. But if you know this business is all rot,

how is it you don't like a particular house because
it's said to be unlucky? You've shirked that
point.'

'I don't like that house. And then—do you
think I'd go and be a servant to be ordered about
by that woman? Not likely. There, now, I'm
speaking in a way I ought not, I suppose, and
making you think me low and ridiculous—which
I have a good reason to be.'

'Why don't you like—Mrs. Vane?'

'Because I don't.'

'All right. We won't dispute that. I say, do
you ever read any books?'

'Yes. I like books when they're nice. But
I've only got one or two. Grandmother can't read
—except the future, you know—and books ain't in
father's line much, he says.'

'What have you read lately?'

'Well, I've read "Lady Audley's Secret"; that's very good. And "The Crime of the Opera House." There's a lot in that I don't quite understand, but that's because I've never lived in a big town. And it's supposed to be in France, too.'

'Quite so. Well, here we are at your stile. If you like, I'll lend you a book or two. I dare say I've got some you'd like.'

'Oh, if you would, I'd be awfully pleased! And I'd take great care of them.'

'Very well. Will you be here this time to-morrow? Then I'll bring 'em along.'

'At this stile?'

'Yes. It's getting towards half-past nine now—say nine to-morrow.'

'All right; I'll come. I must say good-night now.'

'Good-night!'

And the girl put her strong slender hand in his for a moment, and then disappeared into the darkness of trees beyond the stile. It was still just light enough for him to admire the ease and rapidity with which she surmounted a stile, which would have been found a rather trying obstacle by most ladies. And then he climbed the wall into his own premises, and strolled home, whistling, feeling he had rather neglected his guest, but nevertheless, on the whole, rather pleased with himself, with the chivalrous *grand seigneur* feeling as yet unevaporated.

CHAPTER IV.

STEVENS ON CRYPTOGRAPHY, AND OTHER MATTERS.

THE same evening sunshine which slanted through the long narrow hexagon panes of the oriel western window of Sir William Long's dining-room, and made crimson and golden dancing spots on the cloth beyond the glasses of claret and hock, and lit up the lilies and made rosier the roses with which Miss Long had given grace to that loyal table, was much at the same time casting a coppery radiance on the countenance of Pat Vane, as he beamed at the head of his own board in the dingy old white-panelled refectory of Crowhill, a room miscellaneously but picturesquely adorned with South American mats, fans, and whistling earthen water-pots, a fair quantity of outlandish weapons, and a few 'ancestors by purchase' to fill up space, and to be described as the old Kings of Connaught, as the twelve Cæsars or the Nine Muses, the Seven Deadly Virtues or the Sons of Scæva the Jew, according as the humour came to Patrick's mind. Poor Vane was, as has been hinted, not improved by the lapse of time, by prosperity, and by the fire-water of the pale-faces. His body had lost its activity and slimness; his cheeks were more fleshy, the carnations had a purple tinge, and the blue eyes were duller, though a quenchless fire smouldered somewhere behind them. His head and eyelids had a way of twitching sometimes, which suggested a complaint called *chorea*, but he was still a cheer-ful soul, and still firmly believed that the wife he won in his last war was worth more than all his other spoils.

She sat opposite to him now in a black-lace frock, with a yellow rose in her hair, and smiled and sparkled. On her right sat Ronald Macgregor, lank, grim, and desiccated, unaltered by the years, now a Brigadier-General and Knight of several obscure orders. What he had been doing for the last five years few people knew. Some say that one of the native Rajahs had had a chief of the staff who talked Hindostani with a peculiar accent, and provided his Highness with a mysterious and delightful drink, which he sold at a diamond or ruby a bottle, the secret of the making of which was in the bosom of the gods who dwelt in a part of Paradise called Dan-di.

Others had heard of a Thibetan theosophist who was entertained in the mansions of the great in

several European cities, and told people at great
length all about everything, and what they ought
to do, and received messages from the bottomless
pit. There were gipsies, too, in many places who
had foregathered with a strange tall lean man who
rokkered the old *jib*, and knew many charms, a
very valiant trencherman, and well acquainted
with all little games, including such as may be
played with horses. However these things may
be, here he sat in evening-dress at Crowhill, and
next him sat a massive, hard, thoughtful man, who
was Captain Doherty. They talked of old times,
more particularly of the sack of San José, and the
way they went down to the sea that memorable
afternoon, and the two bachelors assured Mrs. Vane
she did not look a day older since then. Captain
Doherty *said* he had been acting as a special
correspondent in Boerland, in Bechuanaland, and

in Mahdiland. He was a fine rich brown, the brown of coffee-berries very slightly roasted, and seemed in good condition.

On the other side of the table, on Mrs. Vane's left, sat the other guest, the small pale man with the straight black hair, the sharp eyes, and the waxed moustache, whose name was Stevens— Edmund Stevens. He had been introduced to Doherty in Paris, as one sent over on a high confidential mission from certain people in America to report on the organizations and to advise. He had expressed a desire to come over with Doherty on this occasion, and Mr. Heffernan, in Paris, had said: 'You'd better take um with ye, Mike. He's high up in—the thing over there, you know, and quite on the inside track. And maybe he has some money to give us. Kape safe, and give me lov to the boys.'

And Mr. Stevens conversed with Mrs. Vane on Paris, and art, and dresses, with an accent that was slightly foreign, but with a more refined selection of words and phrases than those used by the other men. At the conclusion of the meal Mrs. Vane lifted her glass of champagne, looked round at all the men with her beautiful eyes full of feeling, and lit with a smile of triumph, and said: ' Before I go, you will drink with me one little toast—yes ?'

The men looked at her expectantly, and grasped their glasses, which Lee solemnly filled for them. Those two good old war-worn plotters, Doherty and Macgregor, were both in an innocent, boyish way in love with Pat Vane's pretty wife, and would have drunk any toast at her bidding, and marched to the Pit of Sheol in extended order for her sake. Vane himself was very proud of her, of the admiration she attracted, and of the thorough way in which her romantic and intriguing little soul seemed to throw itself into his patriotic projects. The fact was she liked acting. She liked to take the attention of all the men present by one bold yet graceful stroke. And when she said, 'Ireland a nation!' they applauded the fairy figure with the saucy smile, the yellow rose and the sparkling wineglass wildly, and she escaped from the room while Vane and Doherty gave a whoop which woke the rookery. Stevens smiled. Before his hostess had left, she had intimated to him that if he got tired of talking politics after dinner he would find her in the garden. And Stevens thought that would be more amusing than listening to what he was pleased to call, in his mind, drivel about hillside risings.

Lee then put a decanter of whisky, cigars,

matches, ash-trays, and so forth on the table, and left the room.

'Now, boys,' said Pat Vane, 'mix yourselves a drop of drink according to your fancy, light up, and let's get to business. I asked Mac to meet you, because I thought we'd like to have the benefit of his long cool head, as well as the pleasure of his company.'

'Delighted to meet General Macgregor, I'm sure,' remarked Mr. Stevens.

General Macgregor bowed solemnly and spake no word. Doherty rolled his cigar round and round in the corner of his mouth under his moustache, and gazed apparently at a fly on the wall.

Vane proceeded:

'I'll do well to read you a letter I've had from Heffernan, which I found here on my return this afternoon. It took me a big while hunting after the key of the çoipher, and when I got it, it was in three separate spills, and I'd used half a one to light a cigar.'

'You're a born conspirator, Pat,' observed Doherty.

'Am I not? Guy Fawkes, rest his soul! wasn't in it. Well, Heffernan says the order of the day is to hold on now, and go slow, till the elections are over. In the meantime to help at the elections, and cultivate friendly relations with the English political agents who may be useful—and wait for the blooming cat to jump, more or less. Any untoward discovery now would have the worst possible effect on the Constitutional Agitation. The boys in Ireland have had the tip to aisy down and not play the goat. An' I'm a Tory and a Primrose Leaguer, and you're to chum with English Protestant teetotal Nonconformists, Mike, and the Gineral's to preach peace at any price.'

And Vane passed the letter to Doherty, who looked at it carefully, nodded, and remarked :

' Written two days after we left Pahrus, I see.'

Then he handed it to Macgregor, who looked at Vane, who was twitching his head and blinking, as he did when the least excited, and at Doherty, who was chewing his cigar gravely with an expression of inconceivable blankness. Macgregor said, after a lengthy pause :

' It's a verra warm evening.'

' Will you allow me to see Mr. Heffernan's letter, sir ?' said Stevens mildly.

Macgregor handed it over the table, and Vane observed :

' Ye know it's in çoipher.'

'Quite so,' said Stevens, looking at the letter, and making a few marks with a small gold pencil-case here and there. Then he looked up with a smile, and said mildly: 'You know, gentlemen, this is a fool of a cipher. Do you really imagine that even the English Government is so stupid as not to be able to get this read in five minutes? It is simply the alphabet reversed. Z for A, Y for B, and so on.'

Vane and Doherty looked at each other, and the latter nodded gravely, meaning to imply:

'Yes, he's a cute boy, is Stevens.'

Stevens continued in his mild lecturing manner:

'I reckon the cardinal principle of a cipher correspondence is like that of social morality, not to get found out. When constructing one, it is good to remember that what an ordinary mind can imagine, another ordinary mind can imagine too.

Most of those cipher messages appearing from time to time in the agony columns are constructed evidently by very ordinary minds, and are generally analyzed with the greatest ease by an intelligent person. They nearly all have the same weak point, a symmetrical distortion of the alphabet. I've read them sometimes for amusement.'

'Well, what ought we to have, then?' asked Doherty.

'*Now* you're talking,' replied Stevens, apparently using the slangy phrase rather out of consideration for his audience than because it was natural to him. 'Adopting the principles which I have had the honour to lay before you, we ought to have a cipher which is not explicable by a symmetrical system, such as an alphabet, at all. I assume that an obscure foreign language, not usually understood by educated English officials, such as Magyar or Basque, is impracticable. That put into a good cipher would work prettily, if anyone understood it.'

'Mac knows Thibet-talk,' said Vane.

'But Mr. Heffernan does not, in all probability. Irish is objectionable, because the police can find plenty of people to talk it, even among themselves.'

Observe, Edmund Stevens always avoided rhetorical descriptions. He did not call the police 'Castle bloodhounds' or 'bludgeoning assassins.' He liked to call things by their correct names. His accurate, slightly pedantic manner attracted General Macgregor's attention, and General Macgregor thought, 'This man has more than the collective heads of several pairsons.'

Mr. Stevens pursued his lecture :

'Therefore let us assume English to be the

language. Now, there is the cipher in which the essential words are placed in a particular pattern, and then connected up with a rigmarole of other words, and revealed only when a perforated card is placed over them. The objections to that are: first, that my esteemed friend Vane would perhaps light a cigar with the clue in an absent moment; second, that some person might find it (an objection applying to all portable keys); third, that some word might be so conspicuous as to lead to discovery of the rest. There is the system where each correspondent counts pages, lines, and words in a book agreed on; but that is dilatory, cumbrous, and the book might not be at hand when wanted. The best kind of all is that of which the key is carried in the head, like a language which has been learnt, so that one can write or read at any time and place, without having recourse to consultative apparatus. I suggest this, that an arbitrary selection of words be made—short, one-syllabled words, to be learnt by heart, each word to represent a letter of the alphabet. If it would assist memory better, take the first twenty-six words of some well-known song. For instance, "The boy stood on the burning deck"—here "the" is A; "boy" is B, and so on. The word "cab" would thus be "stood the boy." This will only do for short messages. For long messages have a similar arbitrary alphabet made of letters or numbers, only mind you don't separate the words. Run them all together. The rock these things split on is separating words. Any fool, with practice, will spot your "to" and "at" and "it." Remember there are only two letters in English which are words, I and A; wherefore when you see a sign alone in a letter or number cipher on an alphabetic basis, it is either I

or A, both of frequent occurrence.   Then you get
" at " or " it," and they give away the whole bag
of tricks, as Captain Doherty would say.   Write
out your words or numbers, or words and numbers
mixed—that's a compromise to avoid prolixity and
help memory—and learn them by heart ; then burn
the writings.   Talk to each other in the cipher
language till you are quite at home.'

'It'll be a blasted steep thing to learn, that
cipher,' commented Doherty.

'Very likely.   I'll coach you.   My dear sir, you
have a cause at heart.   What is worth doing for it,
is worth doing well.'

' Sure, you're right there.   Every time.'

' Remember a large cistern can leak through a
very small hole.'

'Ye're having nothin' to drink,' said Vane.
' Pass your glasses.'

They did so, after which it might be observed that Doherty and Macgregor consumed theirs slowly and gustatively, yet surely, that Vane took his more frequently and in larger sips, while Stevens' glass was not much lower when they were all three empty than when they began.

'Now I would like to ask,' said Stevens, 'what plans you have, if any, for a demonstration in force, when necessary, against the enemy.'

' You'd better ask Mac about that,' said Doherty; ' he's been in England working, while I've been in Pahrus.'

'By the way, Doherty, that reminds me. Are you aware that you are liable to arrest over here as a convicted felon?'

'I am. What about it?'

'I only meant to suggest that you oughtn't to remain long.'

'Who the devil's going to know um?' said Vane.
'He was only a slip of a lad in those days, and
twenty years' knocking about the world alters a
man a lot. I know it has me.' And he drank
grog again, and added with some of the old fire in
his rather dulled blue eyes: 'The British Government could run us all in, if they knew as much as
we do. Each of us three is, I suppose, an outlaw
here. I don't know whether you owe the Queen
anything, Mr. Stevens, but that's your own funeral.
But us three—Mike, Mac, and poor old Pat Vane
while he lives—will hang together, if there's any
hanging to be done. If everybody was always so
blamed cautious about their own skins, nobody'd
ever win anything. Mike and Mac and me have
looked in the face of Death together laughing,
under nearly every flag in the wars of the world
except our own, and when the time comes we'll

be there, risk or no risk! Mark you that, my
son.

> ' " One day we'll stand
> With sword in hand
> To fight for dear old Ireland." '

'Pat, hold on, dry up, and go slow.   Mr. Stevens
is only speaking common-sense, but he don't wholly
catch on to the fact that we don't use it,' said
Doherty, patting Vane gently on the shoulder with
a large brown paw.

Then General Macgregor took up his parable for
the first time, and said :

'May I ask, Mr. Stevens, what is the precise
nature of your mession here ?'

'I think Captain Doherty and Mr. Vane will
satisfy you as to the genuineness of my credentials,
General.'

'A'm noht dispiting it.   I ask, what is the

precise purrpuse of your mession to us, just now?'

Doherty looked on and listened, silent and thoughtful, as usual, with a fresh cigar. Vane stared vaguely before him with both elbows on the table, and his chin resting on his knuckles, and twitched.

'Well, mainly to ascertain the exact stage of readiness to which things have been pushed.'

'Ay? Just that. And having ascertained that?'

'Then I shall go back and report. That is, if I am not instructed to remain and help to organize on this side of the water. I shall probably get instructions about that after the elections.'

'Thank you.' And General Macgregor sipped his grog. 'You were going to ask me something?' he added.

'Yes; I was about to ask, what have you done in the way of—well, arms and ammunition, for example? That's important.'

'Well, ye see, Mr. Stevens, things are noht in a mature state, and it appears that we are to give up the idea of physical force in favour of the Constitutional movement. Moreover, your friends have noht been precizely lavish with money. Have you brought any?'

'I am intrusted with the distribution of a small quantity of the fund. But I should have thought that you might have stored a few stands of arms, or rigged up a laboratory somewhere to turn out a few cakes of soap—catch on? This old house now, for instance.'

'Surr, I am a soldier, and not a mere assassin! In any case I would not be a consenting party to using the house of my friend Vane for matters which might bring him and his into peyr'ls of the kind you suggest. Your friends ought to be satisfied by this time that they have wasted dollars enough in explosions carried out in the way only cowardly eediots of civilians would think of, and in paying the hotel expenses of American lawyers, who never opened their mouths in an English Court.'

'Taking all the facts into consideration,' added Doherty, 'that physical force is held over for the present, that there don't seem any cash flying about, and that Pat is getting too drunk for political discussion, I propose that this debate be adjourned, and that someone gives a song. Do you sing any, Mr. Stevens?'

'No, sir. But I must say, gentlemen, you have an offhand way of discussing serious matters.'

'We have that,' replied Doherty coolly, and when Vane began to sing,

'' 'Tis the most disgraceful country
    That ever yet was seen,
  For they put their trust in dynamite
    And nitro-glycerine!'

Stevens rose and said :

'Well, look you, I'll take the liberty of strolling in the grounds. I fancy the forenoon will be a better time for talking.'

'Have another drink before you go?'

'No, thanks.'

'All right. See you later.'

And Mr. Stevens left, inclining to the conviction that the three plotters had better be conveyed to the nearest asylum, to seek better entertainment.

When he was gone the trio in the dining-room drew closer together : Vane woke up from his incipient intoxication, Macgregor shut the window and sat down again.

' " The boy stood on the bornin' deck," ' said Doherty meditatively.

' A large cistern can leak through a small apurrture,' observed the General.

' We're to write exercises in blasted Volapuck, and he'll coach us.'

' The lecture on the theery and prahctise of cryptographic correspondence will be repeated, D.V., every Friday evening.'

' The cardinal principle of everything is not to get found out.'

After a few more of these versicles and responses, Vane interposed : ' But he's a clever little man, too. He must have taken Heffernan in.'

' He did. Heffernan believed in him when I left Pahrus. He must have heard something since.

Maybe he'd a cable. Any way, he was only just in time.'

'Are ye sure now he didn't spot the sign?' said Vane, 'for he was turning and fiddling the letter about a lot.'

'He's a whale on ciphers, but I think we can see him and go a hundred better. This is a matter of life and death, mind, and if he had caught on that blue ink, and the alphabet backwards, constituted the whole message—and what message—that little man would be cutting record toward the nearest railroad this minute. By the way, how near *is* the railroad?'

'About six miles. Hilly road.'

'Hour and a half at least, walking with one's kit?'

'More. I should give an hour and three-quarters. There's a pub on the way.'

'Listen now, boys, while I tell you! It is allowed that I'm in supreme command of this show, I think? Very good. Now, these are my general orders. Pat, you will destroy that letter right now, in case our little friend wants to see it again. And you will please send word by a trusty hand—Lee for choice—to give the yacht's crew the straight tip not to let themselves be drawn. They are to get the cutter under way soon after sunrise, and take her anywhere out of sight—round the next headland will do. I'm in her, gone back to France, do you see? having digested that warning about being liable to arrest as a felon, when he misses me to-morrow. Where's the time-table?'

'Here,' said Macgregor, taking an 'A B C' from the mantelshelf.

'Thanks. Let's see, what's the name of the place here?'

' Shervil.'

' Shervil. Sandringham, Tynemouth, Torquay, Sidcup—passed it now—here we are. Shervil. Last train for London 10.18. Great Scott! it's twenty to nine now. Can I do it, Pat?'

' I could not. Maybe you can.'

' You can do it, Mike, if you go soon,' said Macgregor, ' and take Lee with you. He'll know the short-cuts. I've come over that line of country this afternoon, and the driving road is circuitous, owing to the physical conformation of the country.'

' Then don't forget to warn the yacht now, Pat. I'm gone to France, mind, as I said before, and the yacht to keep out of sight for a day or two. I'll go to London to Katey Hynes's, you know, and take up my old quarters in the top room there, and I'll meet what's his name, Dr. Bogimann—Pohlmann, I mean—and stop him in London till I hear the coast's clear here. And I'll warn all whom it may concern. Mac, you'll go back, but not too suddenly, to the place from whence you came. The police can't run *you* in, because that little swine's got no evidence against you. Got a nice room for Pohlmann, Pat?'

'Fine big attic. I've got some of the boys to knock up a long counter, and a lot of shelves, and put a good lock on the door.'

'Bully for you! That outburst of moral indignation of yours, Mac, was really toney. I want to talk to you, but there is no time now. Come and see me at Katey Hynes's in a day or two. When you rejoin Mrs. Vane in the drawing-room, if I'm asked for, hint delicately that I was so drunk that I was sent to bed. Stevens thinks us three about the juiciest assortment of prime fools he's ever struck. The longer he keeps up that illusion the better. You sing to him, Pat, and you prose to him by the mile, Mac, till he wants straws and a padded room. He's a great idea of himself, I can see, so he'll find your society not up to his intellectual level when there's no information to be had, and then he'll go. Mind he's looked after when he does. Now send for Lee, and I'll make him understand everything in no time at all.'

Lee answered the bell.

'How are you, you old thief of the world?' said Captain Doherty; 'you're looking well. There is a hit like a horse's kick left in you yet, I see.'

The tall picturesque, wiry ruffian grinned, and said:

'What can I do for you, Captain?'

'Where's Mr. Stevens at this minute?'

'Walking about the garden with Mrs. Vane.'

'All right. Now you've to come with me for a

little walk. · I'm going up town on the cars. I'll tell you all about the trouble as we go along—and I don't want to disturb Mr. Stevens by saying good-bye! Catch on?'

'*Auvo, Rya.* I'm awake. I spotted him for a wrong un soon as he come. *Dekkimengro.*'*

'How? What's that?'

'When you thought he was dressin' hisself for dinner, he was pryin' about the house, tryin' to drore a plan of it in his note-book, and peepin' in at doors. I never let on I saw him, you know, Captain. But I can tell you what he is: he is a regular black *Romnichal*, of the wrong sort. B'longs to some foreign tribe, likely, and has picked up a bit of education somewhere. *Rawt-felo*† *posh-rawt*‡ whelp of some swell, I expect.'

---

* Seeing-man—inspector or spy.

† Sanguinary.   ‡ Half-blood.

'We'll test that later, I think,' said Macgregor. 'That idea also occurred to me, Lee: don't you breathe a word of Romnimus in his presence till further orders. I'll sort him. *Dekk'?*'

'Tatcho.'

'Now, Lee, fall in,' said Doherty.

'This way, Captain.'

And the wily old gipsy led Doherty upstairs to his room, where he left our honourable and gallant friend, who changed evening-dress for day-time attire, put on a pair of stout boots, packed his limited 'kit' in an old leather bag, and strapped a South American striped blanket on it with marvellous rapidity. By the time he had done that, Lee had put on a hat, and changed his waiter's black for an outdoor suit, and reappeared, saying:

'The coast's clear, Captain. He's in the drawin'-room now, and the missis is goin' to play the guitar to him. Now, sir, we'll slip it as easy as if he was that silly old *veshengro* * of Squire Long's.'

And Lee led the way through perfectly dark passages and down staircases till, after opening a door softly, they found themselves standing in the summer twilight on the flat, irregularly polygonal flagstones of an old stable yard. Then a short silent walk under trees and downhill brought the pale glimmer of the creek into view, and they struck into the path which was alongside it.

' Now, then, sir, it's the 10.18 train you're after?'

' It is.'

' Then I'll take you over the bridge and up the valley 'cross country, as straight as the crow. One hand each to the straps of the bag, sir, and steady double along this yere level, for we'll have a hill to climb by-and-by. Break into quick time if we

---

* Woodman, gamekeeper.

should meet anybody, though there ain't no fear of that yet.'

And they each seized the bag so as to carry it between them, and the rapid rhythmic tread of their footfalls died away in the overhanging shadows as they went away.

Some time afterwards, in the drawing-room at Crowhill, Mrs. Vane rang the bell for the tray of spirits and water to be brought in, previous to a general retirement. The evening had been some-what prolonged, what with music and conversation, and Mr. Stevens found his hostess very charming, although she had apparently little or no interest in the details of the movement, whether constitutional or physical force. She would talk vague and sentimental idealism about the spirit of revolution and the cause of liberty, but she declined to be interested in repeaters and high explosives.

Mrs. Vane also, with facetious modest apologies and coyness, consented to take what Pat Vane called the 'laste taste' in the world of whisky-and-water.

The bell was answered, after some delay, by Lee, in proper butler's array, carrying the desired tray.

'What have you been at all this while, then?' asked Vane.

'Very sorry, sir; I've bin gettin' Captain Doherty to bed, and he give a deal o' trouble,' solemnly replied Lee, and the company smiled, with the exception of General Macgregor, who was not of the smiling sort.

But he sucked in his cheeks, raised his eyebrows, and remarked:

'A man should be able to take his whisky. Now, Mr. Stevens here, I obsairve, can take a grown man's dose. Here's to the success of your mission, surr.'

'Thank you. Let us say success to our common cause.'

'Ah, you're right,' said Vane. 'One last pious toast before parting—Trayson-felony, and more power to ut! Good old gallows, and Portland, and all the apparatus. Trot um out!

'"Though upon the scaffold high
Or the battlefield we die,
No matter, if for Erin dear we fall."

Give us a bit of an accompaniment, *acuisle geal mo croidhe*, and I'll sing to ye:

"'When the Russian's in Herat, the drums will beat for Pat,
And we'll give England tit for tat,' says the Shan van Vocht;
'And how'll you all like *that?*' adds the Shan van Vocht."

Mister Stevens, ye're havin' nothen to drink, and ye're not singin' at all now. P'raps this will suit ye more:

' " We'll fight fair with the pollis, if they'll fight fair with we,
The redcoats ridin' horses we will fairly massa-cre ;
But we'll hang all informers on the sour apple-tree,
As we go morchin' along." '

Pat Vane always got more marked in the brogue when he was under the influence of whisky. After that, Mrs. Vane drove her husband out of the room with quiet decision, and he was heard in distant passages chanting something about:

' *Is go d-tuidh tu amhuirnin slan.*'

After that they all separated, Stevens being conducted to his room by Lee and General Macgregor. Having seen Stevens safely bestowed, and wished him good-night, Macgregor summoned Lee to his own room.

END OF VOL. I.

BILLING AND SONS, PRINTERS, GUILDFORD.